The Wings That Follow

To Mr Giles
5/5/21

ISBN   9798710652626

For Mum, Dad, Nan and Grandad.
For your ever-loving support and your
belief in me.

Love you always

xxx

The Wings That Follow

Abbie Bryson

...The wind stroked my face as we edged closer to the sun,

the bright orange colours all forming the most gorgeous

sunset I had ever seen. It was as fresh as colours brushed upon

an artist's canvas, a sky of fire and passion...

-Abbie Bryson.

Chapter One

Traversing on a branch investigating through the windowpane, a heavy layer of filth manufactured inside the windowsills; it was wide open. I remembered it would be from a former smoke he had the night before. Putrid smells of weed, B.O and cigarettes merging escaped by the window transmitting tracks of green gas that was sure to strike up disease. Cups and empty glasses scattered on the carpet. Earlier we had learnt his name was Dylan, tall with a lean build. His hair was rough and coated with grease, a hint of a stubble lay on his chin.

There she was. Laying beside him. It was her. Murdoc was right; she was here.

She was beautiful, stunning in fact. Sun-kissed coffee-coloured hair rippled around her shoulders, but she looked skeletal, malnourished and emaciated, the fragmentations of an hourglass figure lay underneath.

Dylan hurled abuse at the TV.

"How fucking dare you! What the fuck was that?! fucking hit him!" He was spitting. Uncivil lines on his face grew deeper, any remains of a heart obliterated.

"Dylan please calm down it's just a film. Please." She pleaded, trying to dodge his hands.

"No! Shut the fuck up! Why the fuck are you even here?!"
Drops of yellow spit landed on her beautifully constructed
face.

"Because you haven't called me for 2 weeks, I was worried that
something happened to you." She had calmed her voice down
not wanting to escalate the situation.

"I'm fine Robyn, fucking hell do you ever stop? I do not want
someone trailing around me all the fucking time. Just go
home!"

"But I-"

Her words were cut off by a hand clutching the back of her
head and forcing her to the floor, she flew off the bed bracing
herself by her hands.

"I said go home, Robyn!"

She scampered out of the room like a puppy being punished by
its owner, I could tell she was ashamed, but something about

her manner told me this had happened before. No looks of trauma presented on her face, only regret and a taste of forgiveness. She lingered at the door glancing at him for a few short seconds then disappeared.

She left the house clutching her head and the side of her face, which had now turned red from carpet burn.

In urgency, I extended my wings and set off to the tree.

I must tell Murdoc.

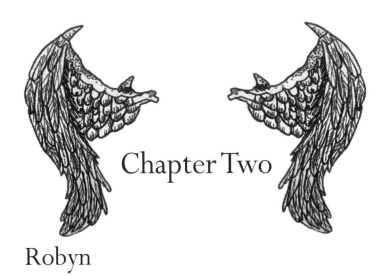

Chapter Two

Robyn

I reached Bernie's just before four, every time wandering in, I could feel a rush of warm air travelling through my clothes and rotating around. Bernie's was a bewildering place, the layout of the building was simple, however, it just seemed that there was a complex passage everyone took. They would veer between tables even if the main aisle were free. Floating above me the vibration of the radio traced my gaze to the TV stationed above the bar on a small shelf, where the teenage employees would normally stand there with their mouths swinging open. I never understood why they even bothered to come into work if they were not going to work. The air had a breakfast smell to it like toast slathered in butter and the sizzling of bacon was hot in my nostrils. Although the food was relatively adequate, they did make some of the best tea, I was an addict for tea. Once I had a Christmas calendar that every day leading up to the 24th I would get a new flavour of tea in the little boxes. Mum loved making personalized calendars to give to us, it was her thing you could say.

I stationed myself in a corner table by the window; the glass had not been cleaned, which was proved by numerous stains of what seemed to be spit and rude drawings in pink lipstick, hearing the seats crackle under my movement, silently waiting for Maisie I admired the carvings and scars of countless initials forced into the tables: A+J, A+F, A+A also a few "*Simons gay*" scrawled beside them. Having only been built a few months ago Bernie's was relatively new. The wallpaper was already stripping, the seats were broken and squeaky. It was empty besides from the hours of 4-6 when people needed a quick and affordable 'pick me up' after work and I heard it got busy late at night. Watching outside seeing if I could view Maisie coming down the slope, I caught a glimpse of myself, my hair was slightly tangled and the back of my head burnt, my scalp red. Not so much as you could notice, it sat just below my skeletal shoulders, level with my collar bone that now seemed more evident than in earlier months.

I knew Maisie had succeeded at entering Bernie's by the abrupt influx of authorization that filled the room as she entered the pub. Promptly the meagre queue retreated up against the wall for her wheelchair like they were in the way of a paramedic, the bitter mutters supplied the muteness. I did not bother to make out what they were saying. But despite that, I knew Maisie secretly relished the attention; so much she could submerge in it. Her wheelchair was relatively new having only been purchased a few months ago. She had persuaded her dad to paint hot pink skulls on the inside of the wheels, despite him being a man of tradition, he accepted. Trundling down the aisle towards me Maisie ordered herself in front of me and placed her hands together on the table as if she were in a conference. Falling over her eyes and lightly trembling in the draft, that had hauled across the shop from the dismal door, was bleach blonde hair with soup-brown roots developing from her hairline that stroked her face and slightly fell past her chin supporting her jawline. She was pretty, very pretty.

"I hate old folk!" She asserted, bending around and glaring at the old man who made it obvious he did not like being moved to stand against the wall with his arms crossed.

Snickering like a schoolgirl being reported a fiendish word I shot Maisie a look. She simpered as she stuck two fingers up behind her back towards the older man before arranging both her hands onto the table, it was favouring to one side, the older man's mouth fainted to his chest in disbelief.

"Okay, okay I'm done!" She spat smiling boastfully, she was fiddling around with her nails that had been freshly painted in matte black with spider webs painted in dangerous white lines.

Half a beat later I inquired "So, why did you want to meet? You told me it was big?" She smirked.

"Well, you know that girl I was talking to?"

"The one with the lazy eye?" I suggested, trying to retrieve all the girls she had told me she had hooked up with or met at a club. I did not like remembering people by their worst features it just happened to be something that stood out in her profile photo.

"Mhm, she asked me out. On a date." Maisie answered, her voice rising in pitch, almost blushing to bring friendliness to her skin.

"Aww, I'm happy for you Maisie, seriously" I gushed, getting worked up and almost blushing myself.

When was the last time Dylan took me on a date? Well, our 'dates' consisted of watching Netflix in his grim flat, that always reeked of fags, and I was constantly waiting for him to come down from his smoke session. That is if he remembered to pick me up. I do miss going out to restaurants and cafés. I felt the corners of my lips shift down my face trying to pinpoint the last time we went out.

"What's up Robyn?" Maisie cross-examined grasping my skeletal hand and squeezing it, she had done it ever since we were kids, it was reassuring, and a hum of nostalgia travelled up my spine and tickled my brain. I knew why I felt disconcerted but did not want to tell Maisie for the fear of upsetting myself, let alone being in Bernie's. The wounds on my heart throbbed as these thoughts progressed through my brain.

"He just forgot to pick me up today" I sighed looking down in embarrassment; I knew I was lying to myself and her. I just really did not want to admit what occurred earlier that day, my face was still sore and red, although I had coated it with foundation. Peeking up, reading Maisie's face, I gathered she was not convinced, she slumped back in her chair.

"I don't get why you don't just drop him, he's beautiful don't get me wrong, but he's…dangerous to you. I mean seriously Robyn when was the last time he made you feel cherished? Loved?" Maisie banged her fist aggravated as she spoke, she had the scent of cigarettes lingering on her breath. She had advised me before, but did not want to admit it, always making excuses for him like 'he's just in a mood' or 'he just forgot'.

"Because when mum di-…he was there, I don't want to let that go. He used to speak so tenderly to me." I could hear my voice fracturing in my throat and gulped.

"I know…and I know what he was like, but You know what. He's a dick." A small snicker escaped my mouth, tranquillizing the throbbing in my chest, whilst wiping the tears away with the sleeve of my hoodie.

"I'm being serious! He is an arsehole. Get rid of him. Get out there! See the world!" she was effectively shouting, waving her arms charismatically; making me snort like a pig as I chortled, spanking the table with my palm trying to cover up the noise of the creature in the room.

"Okay, I'll think about it. If he does not improve, I will leave. I promise" As the words left my mouth regret erupted in my stomach. I wanted to catch these words of regret in mid-air and dispose of them before they were dependable.

Maisie was correct, like always, I had to leave before I got hurt. With Dylan 'getting hurt' would be the safest option.

*

Buzz Buzz Buzz

I observed all eyes scowling at me reaching to quickly silence my phone. It was Maisie thanking me for coffee, sending a quick *no problem :)* I sensed myself smiling, the corners of my mouth upturning. Now with my phone on silent and returning to my drawing, I selected to draw a swift plan of the library. The sun shot rays of light across the floor admiring the wooden beams that stretched overhead. There was the constant noise of scribbling on paper and the clicking from the printer, funny how the library is not silent after all. There is always a low chatter. It is funny how the constant shush of the librarian is louder than all the noises combined. There was a group of girls looking for seats, always glancing behind them before they picked a wooden table to sit at that still shone in the light. They brought out reading books, slamming their books on the tables they began reading. The turning of pages buzzed around the room. The walls were a dark cream with oak wood beams stretching across the ceiling supporting the roof that could fall and crush us at any moment. I sketched the clerk at his desk with the towering levels above, stacked full of knowledge that was waiting to be learnt. This included the amazing mind of Charles Dickens and all the other adventures waiting to be discovered. Sadly, they were just sat on a shelf collecting dust. I have always loved English and art, sketching scenes out of my favourite books. It was my comfort place, my escape. It was the place I could indulge myself in the characters and go on adventures, fall in love. I remember this one time I got so attached to a character I started to try and find someone like him. But of course, I could not. That's the problem with books you get so invested you start wishing they were real. I longed to be in a book, scribbled down on a page and be read to thousands of people. To be sat next to all the greats, have my fairy-tale.

Finishing up my sketch I stuffed my pencils in my backpack, closed my sketchbook and placed it neatly in a convenient pocket.

Walking out of the town library I felt eyes burning into the back of my head, spinning round my eyes met with a girl I did not recognize, she looked at me with the same disdain you would have if you were to step in dog shite with a pair of new white trainers. She had ginger hair strung up in a high ponytail that hung to her waist. She would have been pretty were it not for the line on her forehead from, I presume, staring at strangers on the street in disgust.

Turning back around and quickly walking away I felt a rush of insecurity flood my clothes. She was wearing a white North Face puffer jacket and leggings, whilst I was wearing a maroon skirt, with a missing button, a white turtle-neck baggy jumper and black tights with my favourite black boots. They had, unfortunately, given me blisters until I broke them in leaving permanent scarring on my heels.

I could still feel that girl watching me as I turned the corner almost like I had slapped her and proudly strutted away. Shaking off my embarrassment I hopped on the bus that conveniently came earlier than expected. Sitting at the back window I put in my headphones and started the 20-minute journey home, it was not long, so I only got through a handful of songs on my playlist, some of my favourites by Nirvana and Girl In Red.

Maisie had introduced me to Girl in Red telling me it was the way to tell if someone was gay. Me not being gay and simply enjoying the music I did not understand, however understood it must have been a big thing in the community.

Arriving home ten minutes late because the bus driver stopped at the side of the road and decided to have a fag, I am sure someone will complain. I placed my keys in the small white bowl on the hall cabinet and placed my shoes next to dad's 'smart shoes' he had multiple pairs of these shoes, but he used them for different trips. Walking into the kitchen and making a brew of my favourite apple tea and serving it in my hand-painted fox mug was one of the highlights of my evenings. Our house was not big but not inadequate. The kitchen was a small square, with the sink sitting under a big window that looked out onto the garden, we had astro turf fitted a few years back to save maintenance time, over the years it had become riddled with leaves and had been ripped up in places from the neighbourhood cats looking for mice. Besides, we never went into the garden anymore.

Getting to my room I laid my backpack on my bed by shimmying it off one shoulder before scooting over a mug from the night before to make room for my brew. My room was one of my safe places, I had stacks of canvases sitting in the corner and my finished pieces opposite, I had put a rainbow film over my windows earlier in the year, it made beams of light look like rainbows pouring into my room. I had popcorn ceilings not the most attractive of ceilings, but I try to find the beauty in it. I try to find beauty in everything. As a painter it is my job, my most recent portrait is of a vintage-looking B&B I found in a neighbouring village whilst out shopping with Maisie.

Looking at the pile of cups I had collected on my bedside table I felt a nick of self-discipline and scolded myself, swearing to take them to the sink when I next needed to go downstairs.

Sipping delicately on my apple tea, taking a moment to let the taste fill and warm my mouth before swallowing, I checked my phone for any messages or notifications; Nothing. Dylan had not apologized yet, he usually would have sent a paragraph to me by now, explaining how he knows what he did was wrong and that he was sorry, and it would not happen again. But it always did. Dylan used to take care of me. For the first few months it was magic, but then nothing. It seemed like he had gradually started losing care and interest in everything. It was about three months in when I realized he did not care that Maisie had seen him walking around town with another girl, holding onto her waist and whispering into her ear. When I questioned him, he got angry and started throwing pieces of furniture. He threw a table at me dislocating my wrist, and pushed me out of his house, telling me I was faking it, saying it was my fault he got mad, and if I would have kept my mouth shut none of this would have ever happened.

I hang on to hope. Too much for my benefit. I noticed myself realize that I did not regret what I had promised Maisie earlier that day. He has got one month to prove he cares and can change, not as he would care, I am done with his shit; I am done.

It had fallen dark now; I had just finished watching the last of Kurt Cobain's: Montage of Heck when I heard the rumble of the ocean blue L200 Mitsubishi pull up outside. Dad was home. I heard the door open, then the chink of the keys being placed on the small plate. I pointed my finger up as he shouted "Robyn I'm home!" I smiled as I got it exactly on time, as if it were an achievement, I did this every night. It was a personal tradition of mine.

I ran down the stairs, he was in his armchair as usual his shoes kicked off by his side already. I boiled him a cuppa with two sugars and placed it by his side.

"Oh, thank you, sweetheart." Hearing the low grumble in his voice made me upset, it seemed like he had aged five years in the last year. He had started balding and the worry lines in his

21

forehead became more prominent, he had got plumper since leaving the army. I remember before mum's accident he would come in arms open, waiting for me to run down the stairs he would pick me up and spin me around kissing my forehead. We would all have dinner at the table; home-cooked food. He had got a bigger waistline over the last few months, he stopped going to the gym and had taken on extra hours at the office that meant more business trips, therefore I was on my own most the time. I have grown a likeness to the loneliness, something about it is comforting, it's as if it's the way things are supposed to be for me.

I nodded as he sipped his tea closing his eyes. With him being too tired to remember any of the conversations we could have, I left him to an evening of peace and trotted back upstairs to my bedroom to get changed, this was the worst part of my evenings. Looking in the mirror I placed a hand on my hip. It looked like it was trying to jump out of my skin. My whole

body made it look like my skin was too tight. Although I had

put on a lot of weight since my last hospital visit, I still hated

it. I had promised to eat more and as Maisie's favourite thing

to do was eat, it had helped. Turning away from the mirror I

lazily threw on an oversized t-shirt and hoodie, too drained to

brush my teeth and crawling under the haven of the covers I

noticed I had forgotten to take my cups down; I will do it

tomorrow.

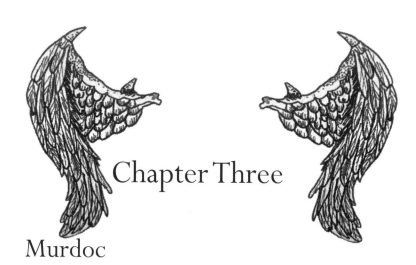

Chapter Three

Murdoc

The springs were a popular place in Enlarnoc, it was a hidden wonder to the mortals. Tucked behind neglected forests and defended by the Guardians. The Guardians were the third in command, they were always trying to enforce the small amount of authority they had been given. They do not even do that good of a job, mortals wander near the springs, they are normal teenagers exploring their new-found freedom. I like to observe them, see how full of wonder they are. I get envious sometimes; envious that they have an end, they can choose where to go, and they do not have to live by the rules of whom you can be with. They can find the right person whatever they are. We get banished for it. My father fell victim. The Second in command were the Warriors, badass, they are tough and not hesitant to break the rules for the ones they love…they would do anything to protect them. Their wings were by far the coolest, enormous rough feathers that darkened the ground they walked on, effective enough to kill a man, powerful enough to carry them over mountains, deserts and oceans that could stretch for thousands of miles. I desire to be like them, it consumes me and makes me want to scream. You must be a full immortal to be a warrior. Could you imagine someone like me being a Warrior? It is laughable. The king is first in command. He hates people like me. He holds all authority over the angels and the kingdom of Enlarnoc, makes laws and anyone who breaks them will be banished or killed. The older folk in the neighbouring villages say he used to be carefree, he was happy. They do not like to say why he changed, whenever I ask, they get unsettled and say it is too much for me to handle, I am not ready.

I know when people lie to me. It is almost like a sixth sense I can feel their tone change and hear them try and think of a defence. See the clocks ticking in their brain. I know it's because I am one of them and I 'cannot be trusted'.

The market boomed with salespeople. Stalls were crammed together, leaving the street narrow, forcing people to walk in semi-straight lines, the cold was almost unbearable, I gripped my hoodie around me tighter. We were coming out of autumn into winter, this was proven by the frost that was strewn about the grass and the minute icicles forming under the jagged rocks. The essence of body odour surrounded me; it was apparent who had not cleaned their wings in a few days, the market was usually like this where the people of Enlarnoc came to purchase fresh fruit and sometimes elixirs from the healers as a treat. The elixirs could give them the assistance of serotonin or productivity, others could be used to treat wounds. Small kids ran in-between my legs, their caramel wings dragging behind them, they were laughing and giggling probably playing chase or something similar, seeing young kids make me smile, the curiosity in their eyes and their innocence, it was like a small spark that dulled as they learnt and grew.

Fruits at the market looked vibrant today, more energetic than the people selling them. However, you did get the odd healer using a scent potion to lure you in. Healers are chill they are mostly hipsters that get stoned half the time 'testing' new weeds and mushrooms they forage nearer to the human cities and villages. There the most chilled people and probably the most entertaining, with their almost heart-shaped wings that stop around the top of their calves, changing colour to mimic the type of drug they are on and with the 'testing' period in full swing, they are technically a moving rainbow. You mostly see swirly greens and purples from the woodland toadstools. It is so beautiful but gives you a headache. Adjusting their fruit and goodies for the market they would paint their fruits in a citra remedy that is used to bring scent blindness back for injured warriors and guardians. I am not sure about the craftsmanship or what is in the potions that makes them do this. But then again, I do know that the fragrances tie to their childhood bringing back a disregarded consciousness.

Why waste money on all this food? That is why I peeped around examining anyone who had their eye trained on me and shifted a pear into my swamp green jacket, the pockets were wide, which was ideal for exchange days.

"OI!" A voice from behind me roared. It was a male temper, middle-aged? Possibly a crafter? Crafters are accountable for amour, machines and buildings. They have all the knowledge of a blacksmith, architect, builder and inventor thrown together. Commonly large built with hands that could grind a stone with a squeeze, they can handle tonnes of materials without breaking a sweat. I have witnessed it. Not the scariest of people but not someone you would want to choose a battle with.

Adrenaline hastened through me. I loved it. I was a junkie for adrenaline. Rotating my head round, I saw that I was accurate, he was a crafter. Big build with petite ginger wings. Ginger was a common trait with crafters. My wings elongated from my back. I took off running, almost losing my stability but snagging a punnet of mushrooms as I did from a healer's stall, she shot me a thumbs up. Brilliant. Too stoned to realize she had been robbed. I took to the sky, my wings knocking over a few stalls as I elevated off the ground and hurried up into the clouds.

"FILTHY HALF BLOODS!"

Half-blood wow so unique, never heard that one before.

I could hear him shaking a fist at me. Imagine having a hissy fit over a pear. Oh! And mushrooms. It was not even his stall. Not my fault they make me pay double for food. What the hell am I supposed to do? They do not let me have a home so how do they expect me to earn money? It's ludicrous, it's a scam. I need to eat. Purebloods do not. They do not deserve the fruit the land has given them.

They do not deserve any of it.

Leaving Enlarnoc and travelling to the tree I flew over Turkey, Ukraine to my right. As the night was growing more sinister the moon decided to make an appearance. Clouds were an immaculate cast of purple and cryptic blue; they were fumbling over each other displaying shadows above. Deciding I still had some time, my wings carried me straight up awaiting the man on the moon who could see me and give me a wave. Relaxing all the bones in my body I let gravity pull me down. The wind biting at my face and my feathers feeling purified. I believed I could stay here forever. Before coming too close to the ground I strengthened my wings to spin around and lift me back up to touch the top of the trees with my fingers before returning to my normal course above.

A few hours later I was just above Germany. The town was so vibrant streetlamps guided everyone, blazing fires roared up chimneys, you could see the livelihoods that lay below. Friends greeting friends, offering pots of stew and home-made soups with thick loaves of bread layered with the finest mature cheese. I could feel my mouth watering, craving the warm comfort that the soup would bring as it would drip down my throat, having bowl after bowl of the bitter goodness. Mortals can be greedy.

Flying over what I believed to be the North Sea, delicately touching it with my fingertips making ripples, I could see the UK coast. I was nearly there. Nearly in England the country of freedom. The one place I felt safe. I felt safer with the mortals than I did with my people. Well, they did not believe I was one of them, did they? I bet they would try and kill me if they got the chance.

I liked being here; I could hear her. Her thoughts on how she saw the world.

Her name; Robyn.

The tree was now in sight, I must have got so lost in my head I did not realize how far I had travelled. The Tree was marvellous. Grand as a tree can get and an old one at that. It has probably been standing here for centuries. I sat in the curve of a branch that had bowed over the years into a sound backrest. Elliot and I would sit for countless hours talking, hoping to find a way we could escape Enlarnoc forever. To sit and come up with schemes and ideas, scribbling them down on the base of the tree trunk since we were on our own. Coming up with a plan was the hardest part. We were all going to go together, but then they found us.

They banished my father. He swore to protect us and that he would find a place for us, but it was too late.

Elliot should be here soon. He would talk about our destiny he had outlined for us. He did not want to interact with the humans as much as I did. Not only that, but he spoke with such passion, changing pitch in his voice was not forced, and with tears falling down his cheeks he expressed how he was going to find a place for us. His passion-fuelled me and pushed the hostility they showed us into a pit of acid in the bowels of the Earth. Elliot was like that, a fantasist. His enthusiasm ignited his eyes until they were the sun. Golden eyes lit the grass he gracefully danced on and flowers rose gently under his feet, growing behind him wherever he decided to go. He was a great friend to the animals, he loved them proven by numerous tattoos he had given himself of the forest creatures. He took care of them and gave any food he had foraged too; it was his favourite pastime. At night deer and rabbits sometimes nestled in his wings seeking the warm sanctuary. He adored them.

I recalled his words from the night before, he had sat at the base of the tree not needing to sit up here with me, he knew; I was listening. I always treasure listening to his stories and concepts.

'... It would have a river running through it! With loads of fish! OO! And we could have cottages with streetlamps to light the way. We could have fields full of fresh fruit and flowers all in nice rows. We would have flowers everywhere. And a library! Every little village needs a library. It would be me and you! Just me and you...'

His words were gentle to my ears and a tender vision full of hope filled my eyes with a dream of a safe place. I collapsed in the crook of the branch wrapping my tremendous wings around me like a sheet.

It must have been around half past two in the morning.

I let the hope consume me and drift me off into an enchanting

sleep while I waited for Elliot to arrive and tell me if he had

found her.

Chapter Four

Murdoc

"I found her! Wake up!" His voice was loud and ringing in my ears, triggering my fight or flight mode. The blur in my eyes cleared as I became aware of my senses. The leaves dangling in my face and the breeze of bitter winds made my body tense and my feathers curl inwards. Bark had been digging into my back leaving aches rattling up my body, my wings felt sticky from the heat I had produced, they made a chewy noise as I pried them from my body like glue that has been smeared between two fingers and is slowly being pulled apart.

Elliot spun to the ground his wings disappearing in a thick cloud of soot. He was panting and had his hand on the tree catching his fall, he stumbled out of the smoke that was immediately carried off into the night by the wind that fooled many into believing that the Shadow man was real. His words rang in my head, bouncing off the sides until they became clear; he had found her. He had found Robyn. I knew she was close! I knew it! Jumping down from the tree like a monkey I ran to him hugging and spinning him around, picking him off his feet and twirled him around like a bad dance recital. My hands were shaking with excitement. I held his head close to my chest, he was smaller than me, it fit perfectly under my neck, he hugged back and squeezed lightly pinching me almost.

He had been gone for a few days, I had suspected that the guardians had found him but was overjoyed that he had returned, and he was safe.

"Where is she? Is she safe? Is she pretty? Please say she is pretty! Never mind I don't care!" I was shaking him to get answers so excited I could feel myself spitting as I talked. I normally was not like this, Elliot was the only one I showed emotion too, emotions were expected but unreasonable. Around the wrong people they make you vulnerable, emotions can be used against you if you show what you are passionate about then they could use that to destroy you.

He brushed the blonde curly hair out of his eyes, it looked a dirty blonde at night but turned a golden blonde in the sun that contrasted with his light brown freckles. His hands were dirty, most probably from sitting in the trees or flying over chimneys. "I've got bad news… she's got this boyfriend a-"

"Well just try and get her to break up with him, they might not last and we'll just wait it out?" I interrupted, I did not like interrupting and I knew it annoyed him, my mind was racing faster than my body, my patience was hanging on by a thread. He sighed and cleared his nose. I got the message and shut my mouth.

"He's bad, he hit her while I was watching and from what I saw it's happened before. And if it has happened before she's gone back, I don't think it's going to be that easy." Rage was bubbling in my stomach and rising to my head turning it red and hot to the touch. She was getting hit. Who did he think he was? I needed to get her out of there. She needed my help. I felt the urge to hurt something. I punched the tree and felt the bark stab into my hand leaving an imprint of the jagged patterns a deep remnant dent had now presented itself in the trunk.

"I need to speak to her. I can't wait any longer." My voice had a tinge of worry as I spoke, pitching slightly, I had been trying to find her for months. I was so close but then the guardians started to get suspicious leaving Elliot to be the one to try and track her down for the last few days.

"You need to wait for her to let you in, she'll get scared and block you out. You could make her think she's going loopy, wait for her." An indistinguishable tone rose in his voice, it was a mixture of disappointment and anger? I knew what he was saying. Did he think I was just going to spring myself on her? I would introduce myself into her thoughts. I could drop hints that there is someone there, besides, it would not matter as anyone would get freaked out. It was the only way to contact her without getting into trouble. He knew that.

"I can't just sit here and let this happen to her, it's my job to protect her Elliot you know this. I can't meet her in person, so this is the only way." I was trying to sound harsh and convincing; it became a muddle of desperation. I wanted to get going, make sure she was safe where she was, maybe plant a seed of doubt in her head about the relationship.

He rubbed his forehead, no wrinkles creased under his fingers, his face was perfectly smooth yet so sharp. Dark shadows carved his jawline. He looked like he was pulled out of the centrefold of a magazine.

"Go then, I'll be waiting for you when you come back. Don't go getting your heartbroken." Pulling me in for a hug. He spoke with a desire that gave me a pinch of guilt. I was not going to abandon him. He had always wanted to be close to me, he had been since he was born. Besides, she probably would not be interested; it's worth a shot. He knew the chances were slim, he had nothing to worry about. I just hoped she saw- well heard something that she liked about me.

We planned for him to stay here, so it did not look suspicious to the guardians. I often went away to the mortal towns but did not get close enough to be spotted. They sometimes had guardians that used potions to turn themselves into animals like owls or ravens that searched the sky looking to see if they could spot anyone out of line. To humans, they looked like a glitch in the system, they could be hovering in one place not moving or look like they have been frozen in time. I am not sure why this happens, I believe it is something to do with mixed DNA going into the potion, I was told this by Theia when we were at school together, she put forth that you need a feather, fur or some sort of DNA from the animal or thing you are trying to transform into and if the DNA gets mixed it creates periods when they appear as a different animal or are stuck hovering in mid-air. I would have loved to go to her classes. They seemed so intriguing. The best smells seeped through under the doors and the most colourful explosions were done in the field behind the school. Our school was placed at the base of the kingdom, it stretched for miles. It was the largest in Enlarnoc and had the highest success rates, kids from all over the kingdom attended this school. I was put into the bottom set, not because of my scores but because of what I am; they made it obvious we were not wanted in the kingdom, they should not have to treat us like one of them. I would stare out of the window endlessly picturing myself high above the trees spinning, twirling, dipping and shooting back up again. I wanted to be free, although I was not bound by the rules of the kingdom, I was still in danger of being punished.

I set off at around four Am, I told him I would scope out the situation and analyse her for a few more days, then I would talk. That was the scariest bit. I had heard that someone had fallen in love with a human and when he tried to talk to her, she went crazy and started tearing her own hair out. She got sent to a mental hospital, and he fell into a deep depression. I took this story with a pinch of salt.

I shook the thought out of my head, I suppose that was the worst-case scenario now that I think about it. This story was told by the same guy that waffled on about his dad who was a billionaire in the mortal towns and supposedly owned Coca-Cola.

Clouds were dancing in the sky clearing the way below, no streetlamps were on, yet you could see the early morning dog walkers and runners claiming the streets, wrapped up in cosy jumpers and coats. I imagined they had some place to be and that is why they were up this early, or maybe they just enjoyed the peace of the morning. There was something safe about walking in the dark in the morning. I believed the dog walkers felt safe with their four legged friends, I had never met a dog, but it was something on my bucket list. I could just imagine how fluffy they were they always looked so happy, but the big ones scared me slightly, they did not scare me as much as the little things with pointy ears and whiskers I cannot remember the name of the creature however Elliot would take me into the woods and show me all different kinds of animals. Only wild animals that is, nevertheless, my favourite would have to be the deer, they just seemed so delicate.

As I got closer and closer to Robyn's home it seemed the fog had taken over and the sky looked sick, a pale grey resting and looking down, its eyes sorrowful. The clouds seemed to wrinkle now and turn a dark grey colour whether it was from the pollution or rain you could not tell them apart. Heading into Robyn's town it seemed she was living in the more working-class area; bus stops crowded every street and it seemed as though she was the only one asleep in her house at this time in the morning. Every other street on the house had people leaving for work, getting in cars, waiting at bus stops. A car was missing from her drive, I presume it was her dad's, he worked a lot and came home at irregular times. Robyn had the same routine almost every night. She would normally spend the evenings listening to Nirvana or watching the 'Montage of Heck' documentary over and over again or occasionally painting. When her dad came home, she would make him a cup of tea and then go back to bed. She was thoughtful and gave the impression that she always put others before herself but that seemed to result in her getting hurt.

Dylan did not come round to her house that often; she would always be at his house. He seemed to not like her house if there was a chance of her dad coming home, that did not sit right with me. My instinct was off when I first saw him hanging out with Robyn, he seemed okay but now we know otherwise. Having said that, I did not know they were in a relationship, or I just did not want to admit it.

I perched myself on a tree that was conveniently placed outside her window, she had the curtains closed, but the window was slightly open, the thought of going in was taken with common sense. It was risky although if I was discreet then I should be able to stay for a few minutes at least. Either way the sun would be coming up soon, so I made my decision.

Scoping the area and making sure no one, or *nothing*, was watching I edged her window open a little more. A gust of wind blew her curtains up revealing a beautiful face gently resting on the pillow, she pulled the covers higher over her to shield herself from the sudden cold. Holding the ridge at the top of the window I slid myself in, my wings dragging behind me, I held my mouth to stop myself from grunting as the tail of my wings got caught on the key hook, sharp pain pierced my body as I teased my feather off. I should have put them away before I came in here but remembered the dust would have been a signal to any ravens nearby that something was not right. Tiptoeing across her floor I proceeded to sit at the end of her bed, carefully looking to where the duvet fell flat, and sat by her feet. She was smaller in person, reaching around 5,6. I was smiling as I thought of her standing next to me. I am guessing she was around the same height as Elliot, maybe a bit smaller by a few inches. She was sleeping like the falling of an axe. It appears she was smiling; the corners of her mouth were upturning slightly as she dreamt, I am guessing she was having a good dream. I wanted to know what she was dreaming about, I wanted her to wake up and tell me about the adventures she had or the people she had met. In our sleep we are limitless, it is a weird concept but also an amazing concept, we can meet past lovers or people we have never met and go to places we have never been. There is a warmth to the silence of sleep, a comfort. Whether we wanted to sleep permanently or not was a different story. Not a choice for us to make but how would we know. Death angels exist alright, the nice ones only come in the night, they hate the thought of taking someone's life while they are conscious. Sometimes while they are carrying them up, they lose their grip and drop you. Leaving you to feel like you are falling, then you hit the ground.

Robyn was rolling over onto her left side, I moved to the floor but peeked my head up to check if she was still asleep. Sitting under her chin were stains of tears. My heart twisted. Her closed eyes looked dewy meaning she must have been crying not that long ago.

The sun was coming up and soon she would be awoken by the beams of light spraying into her room, I did not realize until I climbed through the window that her windowpane was covered in a film that made the room appear rainbow. It added character to her room, the walls were greyish, I am guessing it was not from paint as some patches were darker than others then again it could just be a bad paint job. Her room smelt of apples and fresh cotton, not a smell I encountered regularly. Rainbow streaks were falling on the floor now in parallel lines, it was time to leave. I was grateful I got to be this close to her. To her breathing gently and to feel the warmth of her smile radiating around the room, to witness the softness of her hair. The ravens were probably out now as the owls would clear off to stop looking suspicious, they took shifts alternating through day and night. Getting off the floor as quietly as I could, I crept over to the window, she was facing away from me now.

I do not know if you can hear me, I am going to protect you, Angel, I promise.

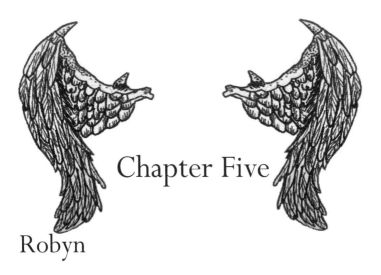

Chapter Five

Robyn

Rainbow beams clouded my vision as if I were underwater without swimming goggles, without checking the time I already knew I had slept too long; the traffic was in full swing, cars were screeching with brakes that needed oiling and the constant honking of horns. Probably middle-aged mums that slept in and are rushing to get their kids to school. They never learnt as this happened at least five times a week, now I think about it that was probably because she could sleep in on a weekend. Well, who am I to judge, why was I judging? This was not like me. Am I normally like this to people around me? I have never wanted to hurt anyone, what was the point? I try my best to be polite "manners cost nothing" mother would say. Reaching blindly for my phone and tapping my desk searching for it like a blind man that has lost his cane. Instead of grabbing it, the force of me tapping my phone knocked it off the bedside table. Grabbing it off the pile of clothing that lay beside me, I squinted to read the time.

Shit, shit, shit, shit.

I was late; very late. I bounced out of bed ignoring the cold that smacked my legs leaving goosebumps to rise all over my body. The window was open, great. It was normally sweltering in here. I ran to my wardrobe and rummaged through and pulled out a black turtleneck and black jeans to match. Then quickly dressed and ran to the bathroom to brush my teeth, running back to my room I snatched my canvas that was propped up on my desk, almost piercing through the material as I did. Rushing downstairs nearly tripping over every step, my feet fumbling over each other with one of my socks hanging halfway off my foot. Jumping off the last three steps before skidding on the hallway floor. I stomped on my boots without bothering to do the laces and ran out of the house, around the corner, down the alleyway and past the big metal bridge to the nearest bus stop, I was begging the bus was still there. Looking down, watching my shoelaces to make sure I did not trip, I heard the bus crawl to a stop.

"Late morning love?" The bus driver spoke, his accent was distinct from Lancashire; it was an accent that made me laugh but not as much as the scouser accent. I opened my mouth to speak but just nodded instead, I was too tired to make conversation besides, he was probably just being polite not like he cared to know. The bus smelt of smoke and cigarette burns littered the chairs. Maisie was supposed to meet me here, but I believe she got the bus before this. Climbing up the steps I felt the blisters on my ankles burn, my boots were not broken in yet and I had forgotten my thick socks. Normally I would have to wear plastic ankle protectors, so the hard leather ate away at that rather than my skin. Sitting down in the middle of the bus at a window seat and looking out the sky was a dismal grey, it had been raining leaving the ground damp. Most of the roads in our area were cracked and potholes scattered about the roads, Aranaville was a mixed town, the rich were rich and the poor were poor. I was fortunate to be in the higher rough ends I guess, despite being heavily polluted, it was liveable. Most people here had frequent bonfires or used old barbecues outside to save electricity leaving the sky to look like a smoker's lung. It tasted like one as the air always seemed thick and sticky. I remember a few years ago I tried to take up skateboarding, it was a cheap set already built, I practised every day. I had been skating for about three months when my wheels got caught on a crack and I went flying headfirst onto the concrete below and grated my face, like a block of mature cheese on a cheese grater, on smashed pieces of a broken bottle that were probably left by drunk sixteen-year-olds on a night out. You got a lot of them around here; you see them fumbling out of the pub or getting kicked out for profanity or trying to start fights. I swear they have no concept of time or what is socially acceptable. I always tried to find the good in these people but after seeing them verbally assault anyone that was different to them or that questioned their 'authority' I decided to just let them be and stop searching, I hope that one day they grow out of this behaviour. Well, I guess it's also the parents that are to blame, but I am willing to make exceptions. Out the corner of my eye I saw a wheelchair zoom down the road bouncing over the bumps, although there was a high risk of her falling, she did not stop. I knew exactly who it was by the hot pink skulls. Maisie was also late. Uncommon for Maisie she was normally irritably early or just a few minutes over time. Maisie told me she had a habit of waking up either very early or late enough that she only has fifteen minutes to get ready, even if she had set an alarm, I guess it just happens to the best of us.

She spotted me through the window and gave me a 'you too?' look. With the help of the bus driver, she was assisted onto the bus before sitting in the handicapped section, I moved up seats holding on to the orange poles that ran around the bus interior and sat beside her.

"Rough morning?" She examined me after looking me up and down, I had not looked in the mirror yet and could tell my makeup from last night had been smudged. Not having time to shower made me feel gross, I could feel the deodorant I had smeared on running down my arm, I wanted nothing more than to get home and start the day over. However, there was nothing I could do about it now, so I might as well make the most out of today.

"You could say that" I was slurring my words, I probably sounded drunk.

"How was your date?" I was genuinely curious; I believe that is why she was late. Knowing Maisie, she probably got her to spend the night. Maisie's charm got her the most out of a relationship. I was still searching for the name of the date, but one could not come to mind. Seductively, a smile crept up her face. It made my stomach wobble when she did, it swam in a circle and then settled again. Maisie knew this. It originated from when we were fifteen or sixteen, Maisie and I decided to play truth or dare, we used different apps to determine our embarrassing or funny fate. It was a breakthrough with our trust, I learned how she found out she was lesbian from a Katy Perry music video, she learned that I had once had a crush on my English language teacher in year eight. We had been playing this game for around half an hour then she had a dare to kiss someone in the room, with it only being me in the room I was the chosen one. She sat crossed legged on her double bed opposite me. Her hair was brown back then but still falling level with her chin. She leaned over, her breath smelt of strawberry laces and was hot on my lips, her lips connected with mine, they were soft and glossy with her lipstick. I was not confused with my sexuality nor have I ever had a desire to kiss someone but at the same time this felt nice, and different. I leant back resting my head on the end of her quilt. She followed and was hovering above me; I could feel her hand gently travelling up my body to my face. Her hand was on my cheek caressing it delicately, I never realized how soft her hands here until now. Her black nails were slightly scratching my cheek but not so much that I minded, slowly her lips parted mine. I could sense she was taking her time to try and make it last as long as possible; I did not blame her. Our eyes locked, not knowing what to do next I let lust consume me sitting up sharply and kissing her again this time harder. Her hand was on the back of my head pulling me closer, the next minute clothes were on the floor and my hands were all over her. After that night everything just went back to normal it seemed as though it did not mean anything, we had talked it over, we established we were amazing as friends, and we were not interested in having a relationship, and I was fine with that. I believe it made our friendship stronger in the thought that we had now experienced nearly everything together.

A sharp poking on my shoulder pulled me back from my memory.

"Ow!" I rubbed the area which had been assaulted by her nails. She looked pissed. I had probably dazed off through her story, guilt pinched my stomach.

"Did I miss your story? sorry I zoned out." I meant it when I said sorry, I hated disappointing her, she looked satisfied with my apology by giving me a smile and gently my stomach untied itself.

"As I was saying! I met Taylor at the café, nothing special, then we just started having the most amazing banter. She is so funny, and she is gorgeous…"

"Wow sounds like it went well then." Maisie was blushing, a warm red seeped across her nose to her cheeks. I have never known her to get this wound up over a girl she has met let alone someone she has only just been on a date with once. She nodded.

I was also relived to know the name of 'the girl with the lazy eye' a name I used out of convenience as I could not remember her real name. I did not want to sound rude or ignorant but that was the only detail I could remember from Maisie ringing me up at four am to say that they had been talking. We were getting close to school now in this short period of time. Maisie had explained how she spent the night with Taylor, and they had some pleasurable time in the morning that she got carried away with leaving her to be late. The school gates were in sight now, our school had a massive budget when it was built leaving it to look royal. The school and the library architecture are what led this town to look so unique.

Getting off the bus, we approached the gates. Maisie and I were both silent, gazing up at the enchanting building. The gates were taller than a double-decker bus; made of steel with intricate patterns running through it. The metal gates looked unpolished and musty, the metal bars curled, swirled, weaved in and out and then back around again in the frame. The building itself was reported to be inspired by castles. Classrooms concealed inside the brick walls were stretched outwards covering a mass amount of ground. It was white under the pandemic quantity of moss that had swerved around the windows and archways. Windows lined the building, they had a vintage feel to them, history concealed in every glass pane. It appears every part of the building had a story, whether that be good or bad people had lived here. That is why it felt so real and alive rather than empty like most buildings that covered a lot of the ground.

Along the cobbled path the double doors that stood to a proud entrance of the school were already open, open to the pursuit of knowledge. However, the archway that held the door was chipped and had bits of plaster laying on the floor. I imagined the people before us had maybe come too early and had lent against the archway with books in their arms waiting to get inside.

Lined with candles the entrance hall looked warm and inviting, soft colours of reds and oranges lit the mammoth corridors, a great chandelier hung overhead, although I have only ever seen it be used in the winter when the sky is darker, and more light is needed.

Making my way to my physics lesson, I parted ways with Maisie once we left the hall and I arrived just as the bell rang. The class was half empty; only a few classmates were in their seats with their planners arranged on their desks. We had rectangular desks that were in rows from the front to the back of the classroom. I kept my head down and scurried to the back of the room to where I was greeted with an icy pinch on my bottom. My Canvas was at my feet as I had not had time to drop it in the art department. It was pointing away from the class only showing the support beams in the back, despite the fact that I was a very proud artist I despised the thought of people evaluating my unfinished drawings. It made me feel vulnerable as you would in an interview for fear of making a bad impression. That is why I would scribble in the start of every new sketchbook to try and clear the thought and the perfectionist attitude. Although I had been with this same class since the start of term I did not talk to my classmates. We did not have any tension or past grudges. I just found some boring, or we did not click with the same interests.

Most of the class had spilled in now taking up the last remaining seats and filling up the classroom. The slamming of books on tables filled the awkward silence then Dr Outen jumped in with a skip in his step and started the lesson.

*

Art was next, my favourite subject by far, with English following closely behind. We were instructed by Mrs Tick to carry on with our portraits working in whatever media we wanted to and to focus on realism, I popped in my headphones and got to work sketching the male's face. The room smelt of watercolours today, cheap ones, probably used by the year sevens, Mrs Tick never allowed the year sevens to use the expensive materials. Not being able to use a reference, which was absurd given our task was to create a realistic portrait, I tried to construct a face from a dream or a memorable face I had seen in town or anywhere for that matter. Laying out the basic shapes was the tricky part then while my paint was drying, ignoring Mrs Ticks instructions on realism, I went to his wings and marked out the pattern of the feathers. Adding horns or wings or even tails was a statement in my work, I believed that every person I painted was mystical or paranormal. After adding several layers to the wings in different shades of greys and dark blues, as black was too dark of a contrast colour, I stepped over to the sink and slowly watched the paint run off the palette, I had a love for this part of art, the paints mixing with the water and watching the array of colours wisp down the drain was rewarding with pleasant satisfaction.

A bang on the window caught my attention and by the sounds of it the rest of the class were startled too, the same girl I had seen yesterday whilst walking home from the library was observing me with eagle eyes, she stared at me with her eyes full of hatred and disgust. She had a line of orange foundation smeared on her face where it had not matched her skin tone. Big golden hoops swung in her ears and she was wearing the same puffer jacket as before, a devilish finger that has probably been used to do the same oppressing 'point and laugh' gesture stuck out in front of me singling me out to her friends, also the rest of the class, and most likely made some insulting remark as her friends (who all shared the same clothing and makeup choice) started snorting. At first mistaking them for abnormally large chickenpox scars I observed redraw hickeys trickling down her neck manifesting their way onto her collarbone then disappearing into her cleavage. She was still banging on the window before miss told her to clear off and get to their lesson. She laughed a hideous laugh almost like a dolphin's chatter outside the window before hurrying around the corner. Feeling the weight of everyone's eyes on me, I kept my head down and sped-walked back to my seat to start clearing away the mess I had made for the last five minutes.

Meeting with Maisie at lunch I told her about the ginger girl that had pointed me out to her friends whilst I sipped a bottle of water I had stashed in my bag. Maisie seemed to already know about her characteristics.

"Oh yeah, that's Brooke, new apparently and a proper sket. I heard she's hooked up down the back of the language block." Maisie shuddered as she spoke, the thought of Brook messing about must have made her cringe. To be honest so did I, down the back of the language block as well? Disgusting.

"I saw her yesterday after I left the library and I think she has a problem with me?"

"What did you do?"

"I didn't do anything; I've never spoken to her."

"Hmm weird. I'll do some digging to make sure she isn't plotting anything."

"I doubt it, Maisie."

"You never know." she threw her arms up to try and persuade her point, and it was working.

"Anyway Robyn, we haven't been clubbing in forever. How about tonight? We could get dressed up and everything!" I thought before I spoke, Dylan would not like it. He would probably accuse me of cheating again, I did not want to go through that a second time. Then again, He still had not texted me since I left his house. The thought made the carpet burn on my cheek tingle. I put my hand on it, suddenly conscious of the slight red tint in my skin that I had not had time to cover up. Maisie had not noticed that probably meant that the colour was becoming less noticeable.

"I can't, sorry. Got homework." It was true but not a good enough reason to stay at home all night, I could have not drunk or only had a few glasses instead of getting shitfaced. Reading her face, I could tell Maisie was hurt that I was making excuses, but I doubted she would try and argue.

"Alright then, suit yourself. Well, it is almost time to leave, so I am going to get a move on and get home. See you tomorrow!" She reversed out from the table and almost into the table behind us before she zoomed around the corner and out of sight into the hallway. After taking a few more sips of my water I strode down the halls that were built of beautiful stone that held folds and patterns like a flame to a wick. I headed to the art department to pick up my canvas that had been left to dry. I decided if I had the energy, I would probably work more on it tonight. The classroom smelt slightly of acrylics and comfort buzzed under my feet. It stood proudly at the back of the classroom prepped upon an art easel.

*

I caught the next bus and arrived home before it got dark. Trying to shake off the dark figure that lay in the trees on my journey home I dropped my keys in the bowl, took off my shoes, placed the canvas on my bed then headed into the bathroom for a well needed shower. After peeling off my clothes into a pile on the floor I stepped in, my toes flinching as they touched the cold tub, I turned the knob that sent thousands of tiny droplets hurtling to the floor and being sucked into the drain. Putting my hand in to test the water first then letting the water engulf me as I step into the makeshift waterfall. The sensation of the steam rising around me and washing the dried makeup off my face was phenomenal.

After my shower, I strapped a robe around myself and made myself a mug of apple tea and headed to my room where I had to budge the cups over to make room for this one. My hair was still wet and was dripping, making me shiver when a droplet ran down my back. The canvas was still sitting on my bed insulted it had not been placed on display. I settled it against my other works in progress when I noticed a small piece of paper folded into the corner of the support beams.

You are not alone do the right thing for you, Robyn. I smiled. Maisie was always one for leaving notes. I felt a wave of gratitude rush through my body as I used some blue tack to stick it on my wall, so it sat with my collage of photos and pages of my favourite films and books. Reaching for my phone to text her a "Thank You" I decided against it and to just enjoy it as is. Hours pass and I find myself sitting in bed with an empty mug of tea re-watching old Disney films when I hear the nostalgic rumble of dad's car. Again, pointing my finger up as he announced himself into the house. He is home early today as he must work night shifts tonight, so he will be off again in just a few hours.

It is around eight when dad goes back to work, and I decided to get an early night. My predictions were right, and I cannot be bothered to continue with the painting. Getting everything out and mixing the paint colours just seem like too much of a chore at this point. I brush my teeth and change into shorts and pull an oversized shirt I stole from dad's draw over my head. Setting my alarm I double-checked my ringer was on and I confidently drifted into my own world 'Robyn's land' as mum would call it. I imagine her sitting next to me holding my hand and rubbing my head gently as I drifted off into sleep.

Adrenaline rushed through me as I sat up alert. Silence filled the room and only the faint rustling of trees played outside. My senses were overwhelmed. I felt as though something was not right and that there was someone in the house; someone that was not supposed to be here. I carefully crept out of bed, making sure I was trying to make as little noise as possible, and peered round the corner into the hallway. Nothing was different, the lights were off only the small beams of light projected by the moon were lighting up the floor. I checked to see if I could hear any sign of someone in the house. Catching me off guard faint snores crept under the door from dad's room, he must have finished his shift early, restoring a feeling of safety and protection. *No ones in the house, you are safe.* I calmed myself and trotted back into my room which suddenly felt very bitter. I noticed my curtains blowing in the wind, I walked over to the window and shut it. Furthermore, I noticed a single feather lay on the key hook, was a bird in my room? Surely not. I examined the feather only being able to determine the colour by the poor lighting. I realized it was black. Studying it closer the feather resembled something like a crow's, but it did not add up, crows did not just wander into windows. I looked out into the night and felt my pulse beating in my ears. A rustle of the bushes turned my attention to a dark figure laying in the trees. Pancaking I closed the curtains and jumped into bed covering my head with the safety of the blankets and forced myself to sleep.

Whatever it was; it was following me.

Chapter Six

Robyn

I woke up as I imagined kings woke, the scent of sweet ripe apples ripped up into my nose in waves of steam, the steam warmed my nose, my lungs expanded taking it in and my eyes were blessed by the daylight. The quilts feel softer this morning, more luxurious and heavier. I scratch the remains of sleep from my eyes before rubbing my head on my pillow breathing in again to taste the sweetness in my throat. My eyes do not feel heavy this morning and I believe my alarm has not gone off yet. Noticing the mug of tea sitting on my bedside table, at first, I am confused. Unless I sleepwalked, I did not recall making this. Positioning my pillows to support my back I sat upright grabbing the mug and placing it on my lap. The warmth seeped through my hands and down my throat. This was not my tea. It seemed to be from Bernie's and had simply been poured into my fox mug. I looked over to confirm that it was not the same mug I had used the other day and had not taken down yet, sure enough my mugs were gone. Had dad done this? I doubted he would have the energy too after working the night shift. I did not dwell on it for too long. Not only that, I just appreciated that he had done this for me, and maybe it was some kind of sorry? Perhaps because he was at work a lot and did not get to spend much time with me. I could tell it was Bernie's as there was caramel sauce on the sides of the cup almost rushed like dad had to leave in a hurry that would not surprise me. I sipped my tea whilst I checked my phone for any notifications, first I turned off my alarm and noticed the message's icon at the top of my screen; it was from Dylan. My heart rate quickened for fear or excitement that it may be a breakup text. I had tried to break up with him before but had not wanted to face the consequences of his anger outbursts. Dylan had a fragile ego, he got into fights over comments made by people on the street, and if you looked at him the wrong way, he would cuss at you. He had done this many times when we were in public leaving me to walk home by myself when he got into fights, sometimes he told me to fight his fights for him for fear of getting hurt. He told me that I made him feel good, that when we were having a session that I was the best he had. I guess that was meant to be a compliment but instead felt like a slap across the face. His constant reminding of how many times he has been with other girls and how many times he had pulled seemed like he was enjoying hearing his numbers climb.

I doubled clicked the text, upon first glance it was a paragraph it read:

Hey babe, so I am sorry about how I was the other day I just got a bit mad and I should not have hit you I know. I have been having a lot of trouble with my mental health recently and my brain has been all over the place. Also, the football's been really stressful this season so that is why I got mad, and it is not my fault. I love you and that you are the only girl for me, and I think u should also stop making a big deal crying and everything about it because it makes my ears hurt and makes me madder, so it is not all my fault. I think you need to stop coming round when you are on the blob bc that means we can't do anything, and it makes me upset. Just remember that you are the best I've ever had, and you are well fit so yeah. So, can you stop ignoring me now and come round or something, so we can have some make up sex ;)

I almost gagged at how pathetic and insulting it was, I noticed how on most parts he had just copied and pasted from other paragraphs he had sent, I read it over and over again to see if he actually apologized or just made excuses. Instead, he just decided to pass it all off and turn it into something I caused. How romantic. Not only that, but I sent back a *'k'* I could not be bothered to deal with his bullshit. If he *actually* apologized for real and admitted to what he had done wrong then perhaps I could get over it, but that message had fuelled me with rage. What a perfect way to start the morning. It seemed that he always had a trick up his sleeve to make my day just that little bit worse or if he was feeling spontaneous; to ruin it completely.

Acknowledging that Maisie had tried to call, followed with a lot of spam, asked if I wanted to go into town shopping. I decided that shopping for cheap lingerie at Primark or maybe splashing out in Victoria's Secret would probably be a good way to get my mind off the Dylan situation, and it would be a nice way for making up after turning down her clubbing offer, Maisie would probably want to know all about it as well, her and Dylan used to be close mates. She is the one who first introduced Dylan and I, she explained how he started becoming really egotistical and big-headed they started getting into more arguments, she detailed how he would start being homophobic to the girls she would bring home and introduced that is when she dropped him. Likewise, at the time Mums' tragedy happened Dylan was there for me through the whole thing I formed an attachment to him, and with every romantic gesture he stuck his claws deeper into me, once I couldn't leave he started letting the romance go, it was a dissimulation he had kept up and he was good at it.

She told me to meet her in town and text her when I am leaving. It was around half eight, so I decided to continue reading my book and finish my tea. One small sip at a time and eventually my mug was empty, I was left with a new chapter to start reading. Springing out of bed feeling productive I carefully put an outfit together, after trying different combinations from my wardrobe, I settled for chocolate brown jeans and a white turtleneck that I paired with my black boots (remembering to put the heel protectors on this time) and a caramel brown trench coat with big dark brown buttons lining the front. I decided to bring a white tote bag with me to carry my purchases and placed my wallet in the bottom holding around 30 pounds and some spare change for the bus there and back. Feeling optimistic I trotted downstairs bouncing on every step and heard dad heavily snoring in his bedroom.

*

Maisie was waiting for me at the bus station in town. She looked like she had slept in her makeup and had a bit too much to drink, common for Maisie and shopping was her cure.

"How was clubbing then?" I questioned as she looked at me like I had just slapped her across the face. After a dragged-out minute she replied,

"I've got a hangover and what I need is some good old-fashioned junk food and a coffee so let's go." she headed to a coffee shop on the corner of an old street. It was midday, but the coffee shop was quiet; only the small clinks of spoons on the side of cups and the quiet murmur of conversations broke the silence. Maisie waved me over to a table in the corner of the coffee shop, I asked for her order and went up to place it and pay. Maisie had given me money to pay her side. Walking back to our seat I could smell the coffee beans being ground and the smell whizzed around the room and popped in my nose. It was slightly nippy outside so the warmth of the café defrosted our faces and left a warm honey glow in our cheeks.

"I got a text from Dylan today." I did not want to engage in small talk, so I went for a different approach. She took a sip of her coffee before answering.

"Oooo what tragic excuse has he come up with this time for not picking you up?" *shit* I forgot I had lied to her about what really happened.

"Oh, um he didn't really give one just passed the blame and then said I should come over for 'make up sex' I almost gagged when I read it."

"So, would I that's tragic." We both chuckled, she had taken another sip at the wrong time and was practically choking.

"Are you alright Maisie?" I could not stop myself from laughing, I felt conscious from the stares what were now set upon us. She stopped coughing and banged her chest.

"Mhm just went down the wrong way" she was laughing now but her eyes had welled up from the coughing. I was still laughing. I could not help myself. Looking out the window I noticed a relatively tall, what seemed to be male build, standing against a building with his hoodie up staring directly at us. I looked around to see if there was anyone else, he could be staring at but there was nothing. He was staring at us; at me.

"What are you looking at?" Maisie turned around and gawked out the window. She followed my gaze to the building but then waved her hand in my face to get my attention.

"Oh, there was someone staring" I blurted, I was not going to lie, she probably thought I was nuts already.

"I don't see anyone."

"Maybe they've gone?" I was trying to make myself sound sane, and also trying to convince myself that I had not seen anyone and if I did then they were not looking at me, Maisie looked happy enough to ignore my comment and dive straight back to her coffee and cheese and tomato melt. She had bitten off more than she could chew leaving her with a string of cheese hanging on her chin. She was laughing trying not to let anymore fall out of her mouth. I peeled the cheese off her chin and stuck it to her plate then wiped off the residue that remained on her chin with a tissue. She was contorting her face as I did this, trying to make it easy for me, but also trying to finish off the bite she just took. I only noticed now that Maisie had not thought about her black lipstick and the effect eating a big meal would have.

Finishing our coffees and Maisie finishing the last of her salad that came with her main we left a five-pound tip and left, heading to the main shopping high street. The cold froze my legs, but I was grateful I had thought about the weather. Maisie on the other hand was near to freezing, she was wearing cuffed black jeans with a spaghetti top and a leather jacket. Do not get me wrong she looked amazing, but it was not thought through. We entered the Victoria Secrets shop whereupon entry we were greeted by the rush of heat flowing past us from the fan above.

"Right, where too first?" Maisie was eyeing up the perfumes and jewellery, whereas I had my eye set on the deals and bargain bins. We cleared most of the shop, frequently questioning why most of the material was missing from swimsuits or underwear. We got around to the bargain bins and discount sections where I really started to dig. I found a red lace thong with stockings to match and an odd-looking polka dot strapless bra that seemed to be missing its matching ally.

"OO this would look great on you!" Maisie exclaimed holding up a black lace bodysuit and throwing it at me. I held it up examining the lack of material.

"No way, I'd look like a skeleton in a bin bag wearing this...you'd look good in this!" I chucked the polka dot balconette bra at her, she screeched and batted it away with the palm of her hand.

"Disgusting!" she looked genuinely upset like she was about to cry. I held the black lace piece up again; it was not *that* bad. I checked the price tag. 70% off, brilliant! I guess they were having a summer sale since they were going to start needing to get more of the festive stuff in stock. I studied it again, doubt crossed my mind about how I would look in it, I imagined myself in the mirror this horrible figure almost spider like. *Buy it Angel, you will look great.*

"What did you say?" I looked at Maisie, what was this Angel name? Had she just come up with it?

"I didn't say anything Robyn." She looked worried as a line creased over her eyebrow. I swear I heard something. A voice, but it was deeper than Maisie's, unless she was doing an accent thing again. The most annoying month of my life, she decided that she was going to try and speak in a Scottish accent, I have to say I felt like taping her mouth shut most days.

Who else could have said it and why did this "Angel" thing sound familiar, not the word in particular, the way it was said, the voice? It pinged in my head like a forgotten memory, a shape I could not grasp. I ruled it out as Déjà Vu.

"Are you okay Robyn?" She was in front of me now with her hand on my shoulder.

"Yeah, sorry I just swore I heard someone" I looked around the store to see if I could find anyone that looked to match the voice, but I saw the same tall male build with the same grey hoodie leaning outside the glass window. The fear that I felt last night, when I saw the figure in the trees came crawling back to me, the same fear I felt when I was on the bus ride home and I saw the figure in the trees. I suddenly felt unsafe. My head felt hot and heavy, and I felt worry boil in the pit of my stomach. I snatched the black lingerie and headed to the tills to pay. With Maisie still wanting to shop inside, I told her that I would wait outside and for her and would not to be long. Walking outside with my tote bag under my arm and the receipt falling out my back pocket, I sped up to see if I could get a closer look at the figure, could it be someone I know? Hurrying out the door and feeling that temporary blast of heat, I turned to find the figure had gone, I just saw them a second go. I felt heavy as I sensed eyes watching me from all areas targeting me like a deer in hunting season.

I heard Maisie come up behind me, two bags of clothes attached to her wheelchair.

"So where to now" Maisie sounded eager, already eyeing up Primark and Poundland. Pushing aside my feeling of worry I soldiered on into one shop after the other. I had only bought three things by the time we were at the bus stop, whilst Maisie had piled high years worth of clothes and makeup. I believe she truly had an obsession. The bus rolled up; the majority were seniors who got off. Maisie and I had decided that we should go round her house for a sleepover as it had been months since we had the last one. I texted my dad on the bus there, and he agreed it was completely fine and that I have his number if I need anything.

We arrived at Maisie's street about half an hour later. It was about a twenty-minute walk from my house that made it ideal in case you forgot anything. Walking up the hill to her house we noticed a group of chavs headed down the road like a pack of wolves. The 'leader' being a chubby boy wearing blue trackies and baseball cap. I could feel Maisie tense, it gave the impression that she had encountered them before, and it was not pleasant.

"OI!" He shouted from the top of the hill cuffing his mouth as he spoke, as if he were not being loud enough, we kept our head down not daring to make eye contact. His footsteps grew louder, hard and heavy.

"OI" He shouted again this time looking over his shoulder, I am guessing to try and get respect from his mates, they all seemed to look the same, fags in one hand and their other hand scrunched into a fist. One had a vape, and he was leaving a trail of steam behind him. I presume it was to look hard or intimidating, it did not, it just made him look like a prick. He threw the fag onto the floor and stomped on it vigorously to make sure it was out; it left a mere scorch on the pavement. Heading in our direction we sped up, seeing Maisie's house coming into view, we wanted nothing more than to get past without getting killed or mugged.

A glob of spit was spat next to my shoe, Maisie and I made eye contact, she almost gagged when she saw its yellow tint. It looked like it had been wrenched out the backside of a cat.

"PUSSIO!" I could feel drops of spit land on my face as he shouted, I wiped it off quickly hoping to eliminate any germs that had now transmitted to my skin. Maisie looked at me horrified as we got to the top of the hill, she rubbed off the residue of spit placed by the vermin of this age with her sleeve. No words were exchanged only a 'fucking hell' stare.

Finding it vulgar when people spat in public, especially near me, I gagged hoping nothing came up. I thanked that the spit did not hit my boots.

We marched up the metal ramp leading to Maisie's house, I had been here a few times but remembered the ramp being a lot sturdier, it wobbled under my feet and made my legs feel like jelly. Walking into her house it smelt like Christmas, like cinnamon and the smell of a kitchen that had been used to make jam for a grandparent. Although we were only now coming out of autumn, I felt festive, I wanted to go carolling or do a good deed or give to charity. Her walls were a vibrant grey and candles burned on the wooden shelves. One smell hit after another: woodland, snow, shortbread, gingerbread and a hint of pine. I let my lungs expand, taking in the array of wondrous smells and let the warmth of her hallway seep into my skin and carry throughout my body like the heat from a hot water bottle.

I hung my coat on the banister and placed my shoes on the shoe rack, her hallway had been modified to help people pass when Maisie used her wheelchair. Walking through to the kitchen photos of Maisie's dads' lined the hallway. I was in hospital when they got married. I was asked to be a bridesmaid but unfortunately could not make it. Maisie ended up bringing me a slice of wedding cake but ended up eating it.

Sitting at the breakfast bar was Mark; A tall man with a sculpted build, his angular chin that could cut through an atom was hidden by a trimmed beard, his black shiny hair was combed back, and he was dressed in a tailored blue suit and shiny brown Oxfords. Sitting beside him, an arm around his waist, Charles rested his hands on the countertop scrolling on his phone. He was a shorter man with a bulky build; he had a shaved head, slightly balding to the top, and soft features. A soft brown suit made him soft to the eye that was complemented by black, and freshly polished Brogues.

"Going somewhere?" Maisie questioned looking them up and down. They smiled upon her entry and got up to greet her with hugs. Spotting me in the doorway they hugged me tightly as if we were having a family reunion.

"Robyn! You're looking so much better, what a nice surprise!" Mark hugged me tighter. It was the same hug he had given me when he found out about my mum. I hugged him back like an old friend, he was a trained psychologist and was my therapist for weeks after the tragedy.

"We're going out tonight! We decided it was time me and your dad got out again as we've been so tied up with work" Maisie nodded in agreement. Charles chucked his credit card on the countertop and told us to order some food for our 'girls' night'. Maisie was quick to grab her phone and search for fast food that delivers. Mark and Charles had left proven by the sound of the ramp ratting outside and the sound of car doors closing.

"Dominos?" Maisie was reading from the list of nearby restaurants, not forgetting the fast-food joints that delivered.

"No, I'm not feeling like pizza."

"Turkish Grill?"

"Nah maybe somewhere more delicate or something we haven't tried before?"

"Marrakesh!" Her eyes cartoon like, and she had her hands together begging me.

"Alright, Marrakesh it is!" I was actually excited. It had been ages since I had Marrakesh but with dinner on Charles and Mark, I think it was okay to treat ourselves. We ordered food and went upstairs while we waited. We stuck on the TV and chatted whilst Gordon Ramsey shouted at cooks on the TV.

Lying my head down, my stomach full, I closed my eyes and tried to drift off into unconsciousness. Listening to Maisie's sleep talk was perfect background noise, like a TV, she spoke of anime and her shoe Wishlist. I smiled, I felt lucky enough to have her as my friend, the night felt peaceful. Closing my eyes, I thought of colours swirling together in different shades and then bursting together again.

Goodnight, Angel.

Chapter Seven

Robyn

Milling around town I could not shake the name 'Angel' echoing in my head, even after checking over my shoulder multiple times I felt as though I was being watched.

"OO how about this one?" Maisie pointed to a 2010 Suzuki Swift. I had been considering buying a car, so I did not have to catch the bus every morning. Public transport was not only unreliable but expensive, you could also encounter a lot of 'characters', once I had seen a gentleman climb into the bus with a plastic bag filled to the brim with raw meat, not packaged, blood was spilling on the floor, it smelt horrific. I could almost taste it, that bus got evacuated and had to go for a deep clean to get the stench out.

We had gone to a car dealership looking for the cheapest price we could snag. I had two thousand pounds saved up, having my driving licence already, I just needed the car.

"It's used and £3,500, not bad if you ask me," I walked over and checked the car, looking inside and out, it looked good for a used car. It was not dirty nor did it have a funky smell!

"I only have £2,000 Maisie; I need a job of some sort." The deliberation of having to wait another few months for a car dwelled on me. Contrarily, I did love to work so maybe having a job would be a good use of time and productivity. Selling painting at the local art gallery was not pulling in any money like it used to.

Over the next few hours Maisie and I cruised around town enquiring at restaurants asking if they had any positions available, most were not hiring or paid so little it would take me years to save up for the car, not even counting the essentials I would have to dip into my stash to pay for. We had got business cards from three different restaurants that Maisie and I were going to travel back to mine to review. I always without fail check the reviews of previous employees that have worked there to see how they were treated and if they had any tips.

Entering Bernie's for some brunch I routinely ordered apple tea and decided to treat myself to a tuna sandwich. Tuna sandwiches were an all-time favourite of mine, to think I used to try and throw them in the bin when mum gave them to me. I savoured the taste letting it sit in my mouth and slowly chew before swallowing. Despite Maisie's slim figure she had wolfed down a bowl of tomato soup that had left a bright red tint her tongue, she was now onto her ham and cheese toastie. It was a classic dish for Maisie and by the time I had finished one half of my sandwich she was onto her second slice of chocolate cake. The cake looked rich and moist, unlike our school 'brownies, she took her time with this cake savouring every chunk. The school brownies were more like sand in your mouth. I completely went off them when I took a bite and heard something crunch.

"So, how's things going with Taylor?" I questioned taking another bite. The soft bread was folding into my mouth and the tuna fell with it. She did not hesitate,

"Perfect, I think she's *the* one you know?" I did not know. I wish I knew, but I never had that feeling. Self-confessed I had loved, but never thought it would be eternal or that I had found my soulmate. Frankly, I did not believe soulmates existed. I thought that believing that they are the one would only get you hurt when things went sour.

"Well, I hope it works out for you Maisie." It was true, of course it was, I wanted only the best for her as she did for me which is why she had been probing my brain for any reason to break up with Dylan. It became clear things were not going to get any better and only worse, so it was time to move on. Dylan had made me go through the stages of a breakup and grief beforehand when he had his 'episodes'. Occasionally, he would pretend to have died by laying on the floor for an unnecessary length of time, hiding phones beforehand or cutting off the power supplies, so I could not ring anyone for help. If I tried to go to the neighbours for help, I was faced with the fact that he had locked the windows and doors. He would sit up, hug me and tell me it was only a joke, and I was being overly dramatic consequently he would say, 'you just can't live without me, can you?' He was right at the time I could not.

Maisie was resting her head on her hand, gazing up and doubtlessly dreaming about Taylor. Was I really this obsessed with Dylan, was that how I behaved? It was not bad; it just left a seed of embarrassment in my stomach. I had almost finished my sandwich now getting to the crusts before setting them on my plate. I had picked at the salad but instead finished my small bowl of crisps. With our stomachs now bloated. Maisie and I decided to stroll aimlessly around town for the second time today. Our town was beautiful, having minimal amounts of things change over the last few decades it looked vintage. Buildings were whitewashed with dark wooden beams lining adding texture and character. The streets were cobbled, and Old-fashioned signs swung from buildings in the wind. Our town had its own blacksmith and a vast church, although I was not religious, from time to time I sat in the church to sketch its interior to use for inspiration. Our streets were undemanding, and maps sat dotted about for tourists. We had cobbled steps and leading down through two whalebones you could walk to the beach. Our town was located near the seafront, excluding the bitter weather. It was picturesque. I had burnt out many days sitting on the beach painting the landscape on a large canvas that hung in a gallery not too far from here. I did not earn much from this shop, near to nothing, but the publicity helped get my small business off the ground. It was a career I wanted to pursue, but my dream was to get into teaching fine art classes or owning my own an art shop in Whitby that nestled on the small cobbled road. I had stayed up countless nights researching prices, and the probability of success; going on tangents of research in the endless pursuit of knowledge that I may or may not need for my dream to have the best chance of success. I would gaze at the screen letting my eyes go fuzzy and my head ache. Only a few months ago I had gone to the library to do 'light research' it ended up with me being woken up by the librarian to be told that I had fallen asleep and they were locking up to go home. She was a lovely woman, and I would often give her a smile and a wave if I pass her in the street or see her at the library. I would like to think she was the type of person I could sit down with for a conversation without it being awkward. After she had found me, she took me out for a coffee with her.

After Maisie and I had browsed the local shops and sat on benches to waffle about jobs or cars, she started repeating everything she had showcased earlier that day about Taylor. She was verbalizing how her skin was so soft and how she smelt of vanilla, frequently pulling her shirt over her nose, inhaling heavily to try and feel the sensation of her scent. Upon it ringing only once she hastily pulled her phone out and with a wide grin now stretching from ear to ear, she stood up and took the call from whom I could only guess was Taylor.

Her voice seemed to zone out as she giggled and twirled further from the bench. She gave me a 'sorry' look and I shooed her away with a smile. She held the phone close and her smile only grew taller. It seemed as though when she spoke to her, she became a happier person, it reminded me that I was only falling deeper into this grave Dylan had created for me. With time to myself I entered my own head to explore the voice I kept hearing, not just in my dreams, in real life too. I had merely shaken off the thought, but now I believed someone was truly messing with me. I kept imitating that name 'Angel' again and again to try and make it sound familiar. What's more is that I hunted for a memory or event to see if anyone had said anything like that to me before. It had never been a nickname of mine. I do not recall knowing anyone who would desire to call me that. A shiver crept up my spine as I pondered if it was the individual, I suspected was following me. Perhaps the figure that laid in the trees was trying to communicate with me. The hair on my neck erected. That feeling surged in my chest again, looking around I was panicking, my palms had become caked in sweat. The figure stooped down behind a tree to my right, I locked eyes on the hooded figure. He was now closer it seemed as though he was taller than me, but his eyes were shielded by the thick fabric hanging over his head casting a dark shadow over his face. With the sudden nerve to confront him I patrolled over in his direction with my fist scrunched in desperation. Acknowledging my presence, he rose and swiftly slipped round the corner, that is odd. My suspicions grew stronger and so did my anxiety. I felt the manifestations of a lump build in my chest rising into my throat, my head was throbbing with stabbing pain on the right side of my brain, I followed him down the cobbled street, and then he disappeared. Advancing further down the street I stared at every possible exit: the barbers, nearby bakery, and the trail to the beach. Bringing my search to a halt I was met with a heart wrenching sight. It was Dylan with his arm around Brooke slightly fondling her side then proceeding up her shirt and with no hint of truth behind his eyes, he was whispering into her ear. Tears flushed my eyes and started streaming down my face. Dylan pressed his face to Brooke's practically sucking her face viscously and then pulled away, he moved his mouth to hers again kissing her aggressively, she leant back against the force of this intrusion. The look on her face told him everything. I doubted they were even dating, knowing Dylan, he only wanted another girl to add to his list. I wonder what sweet nothing is he whispered to her, what promises did he make? Not only that, but I also knew he would promise her the world. Well Brooke, I have news for you.

I had the perception of tears running down my chin and I felt a tap on my hip, long back nails told me it was Maisie.

"OMG Robyn what happened!" I've been looking for you!" she looked like she was about to cry. She hugged me, turning me around, gently wiped the tears away from my eyes and chin, then she pulled me in close. I tried to speak, but only murmurs seemed to fall out of my mouth to hit the ground and explode.

Instead, I pointed to the direction they were in and followed my gaze and her whole body froze. Without warning, she shook me off her and hurtled through the streets towards them. I chased after her.

"MAISIE!" She ignored me; people jumped out of the way for fear of having their toes run over. She stopped herself a few inches away from them and climbed out of her wheelchair, I had only seen her walk around her house for a short period of time, her legs were frail, they had got worse over the past couple of years, she was prone to falling over and if she stood for too long, she would be in pain sometimes it was agonizing hence why she had a wheelchair. Before I could stop her, she had raised her fist and struck him across the nose. His face contorted making impossible faces he tumbled back onto the floor where Maisie walked over kicked him in the head with her platform and she held it there making sure it ruined his pretty little face.

"You are cheating SCUM! Think again next time DICKHEAD" Spitting as she scolded, little droplets of spit sprayed on his face, before gracefully sitting back in her wheelchair and headed back to me. Dylan's face now looked like a can of dog food, he had blood clots falling out of his nose and cuts from where the boot had stamped maybe a little too hard. No one tried to stop her, instead all eyes fell upon him, they glared showing no signs of remorse. Brooke was quick to sashay away, she had a face like she'd just bitten into a lemon her eyebrows seemed to get thicker by the day not to mention it looked like she had also gone with a more tangerine colour foundation this morning. Dylan quickly got up and walked away pulling a hood up over his head to conceal his face and wiped the blood from his nose.

The mix of tourists and townspeople cleared off and broke the crowd that had formed around this occasion, some headed past us giving us thumbs up. Two elderly women approached us, both grey in hair but with the attitude of youth sitting proudly on their shoulder.

"Well done girl, you showed him!" she patted Maisie on the back and smiled gently.

"Well, I would do anything for my friend." Maisie looked at me and smiled with loyalty.

Reaching into her bag she pulled out a two-pound coin and placed it gently in Maisie's palm holding her hand for a brief second before letting go.

"Go buy yourselves an ice cream, both of you treat yourself," she turned to me.

"It's okay love, things will get better" she smiled a warming smile, like a grandparent being visited by their family for Christmas or a mother smiling while holding her new-born close to her chest. They wobbled down the road, looped arms and laughed.

Maisie smiled at me and I realized I was smiling back. Warmth seeped through my chest. Maisie hugged me close, whipping off some mascara with her thumb that had escaped the corner of my eye.

We walked back to the town bus stop; Maisie was smiling to herself.

"Proud of yourself?" I questioned already knowing the answer, she gave me *that* look raising her eyebrow and looking up at me.

"I've wanted to do that for such a long time you wouldn't know." I did know. I wanted to stamp on his stupid little face. But the difference between Maisie and I is that she does it. She keeps promises I only make them. I would not dare to stand up to Dylan just for the fear of my safety but there has to come a time eventually. I am just hoping that he either breaks up with me or drops *dead*.

*

Walking down the steep hill we took notice of white specks falling on the ground, they fell delicately to the floor, as if it were a blanket, soft and warm. Striking my hand out I count snowflakes trickling down from the sky, giving the world a new shine. It tingled for a second as it melted, the liquid that had now formed in my hand ran through my fingers. Rubbing my hand on the side of my coat, we took our time now going down the hill leaving our trails with every step, Maisie's wheelchair left big tire marks swerving down the pavement. I found snow to be like a blank page waiting for people to have a magical time, kids were already fumbling out their homes in big coats and welly boots, they were tugging their mums and dads out of the house who were still trying to fix on their woolly hats but instead dropping them in the snow. Kids giggled and danced about in the snow.

I twirled facing up to the sky letting the snow land on my face, closing my eyes and taking in a deep breath. It was like a moment out of a film. I imagined Sparks by Coldplay Playing in the background, while I stuck my arms out embracing the cold letting it tingle my body and drift through my clothes.

The sky was a much paler blue now and snowflakes were landing on my eyelashes but melting within seconds. The snow was getting heavier, Maisie was already at my door I ran down the hill after her, praying the grip in my shoes did not let me down, I got to the bottom of the road almost running into the bus that stood outside a small bungalow that was now wrapped in a frosty sheet.

Hands shaking whilst I fiddled with the key in the lock.

"C'mon I'm freezing!" Maisie was pulling her leather jacket tighter, her lips were draining of pink, we were both just craving a warm fireplace and a mug of hot chocolate and for the first time in a few months I craved something sweet.

I shoved the key in the lock and smashed down on the handle, my hands burning with the contact of the cold metal, hot thick air hit me like I was stepping from a plane into a hot country. Stumbling into the house, Maisie following close behind, slamming the door and throwing off my coat and chucking my boots next to dad's I slipped my bag off my shoulder. Rubbing my hands together I walked to the kitchen to put the kettle on. "OO yes please!" Maisie shouted from the hallway I could hear her grunting as she struggled with the zip for her boots. Hearing them hit the wooden floor indicated her success as Maisie came through rubbing her hands together, she was still smiling, however the colour had now stumbled back to her face providing the rosy red glow that had stained her cheeks earlier that day after the call with Taylor. I checked the small mirror we have had in the kitchen for years; my makeup had stayed intact as only a few specs of mascara lay under my eyes.

"Tea or coffee?" I called, she paused before answering,

"Do you have any hot chocolate?" I checked the cupboards sure enough there was a small tub at the back of the cupboard, it had not been touched in years, proven by the multiple layers of dust that caked the lid. Placing it on the counter and wiping the dust from my sleeve I make us both a cup and topped it off with whipped cream, flake, wafer, a sprinkle of grated chocolate and a toasted marshmallow that sat peacefully on top of the wafer. I was trying to recreate that iconic drink from 'The Simpsons'. It looked like a disappointment but tasted exquisite. Maisie had decided to chug it trying to get all the cream to fall into her mouth at once but that ended up with chocolate stains down her.

The snow continued now, and thick mounds had coated the corners and bottoms of the windows. The kids outside had gone in now and the streets were deserted. It looked as though my house had been wrapped in plastic. We turned on the TV and the reporter spoke of the possibility of being snowed in, local transportation to come to a halt and schools & colleges will be forced to close if the snow continued to settle. I was not worried, snow did not seem to hang around here instead it would melt by morning, causing minor floods. This normally had the same effects as being snowed in.

Maisie and I had not spoken further about the events that happened earlier that day. Well actions speak louder than words at the end of the day.

"So…when are you going to do it" I was confused at first but then realized she was talking about Dylan, after this incident I was almost obligated to break up with him especially after Maisie had risked public humiliation and getting beaten up for me.

"I promise I'll do it sometime this week or on the weekend if something comes up, but I will do it. I swear." I crossed my heart, the essentials for making promises, then pulled her into a hug whilst trying not to spill my lukewarm hot chocolate down her

She kissed my forehead, the least abnormal thing to happen at this point, and pulled me in again. We headed upstairs after quickly rinsing out our cups and wiping away the chocolate powder that had been left on the side.

Upstairs, I quickly spot cleaned my room. Despite the fact it was not particularly messy, I felt conscious as Maisie had not been in my room for a few weeks. I could hear her heavy footsteps coming up the stairs before she flung herself on my bed. I laughed, I could not help it, it was just one of those things. Maisie started laughing too which sent us both into hysterics. I was slapping my knee to try and stop myself until a snort escaped my mouth. I was on the floor at this point rolling about, my chest was tight, I noticed I was not breathing. Steadying my breaths and calming myself I could feel my lungs untie themselves and settle. Maisie also stopped too having only been provoked by my outburst.

"Who's that from?" I followed her gaze to the note *she* had left in my canvas. I gave her the 'c'mon you know who' look. She raised an eyebrow suspiciously.

"You did?" I questioned now, second guessing myself.

"No, I didn't Robyn."

What? Who could have possibly left it? Multiple questions whizzed around my head trying to untangle this situation.

"I thought you left it; it was in the corner of my canvas."

"As much as I am honoured by the thought you would put something on your wall that I gave you. It wasn't me."

"Then who?"

"Secret admirer maybe!?" she got excited at this though, probably because she could now imagine me with someone new.

"But how would they know to make it so personal? How do they know what's personal?" Suddenly it clicked, it must be the guy that has been following me. He has been spying on me! But why would he try and help me? What did he want?

"I don't know but maybe it's someone who might want to be with you and is just telling you to take care of yourself?" Maisie was trying to be positive, but I could tell she was concerned, I did not have any other friends let alone talk to people from my class so who could it be?

"How about we look through the flyers and see about getting you a job, you know, to take your mind off it. It was probably that ginger bitch trying to play some sort of mind trick, so she could have a chance with Dylan." That did seem like the most likely cause, she did know about mine and Dylan's relationship, and it would be profitable to her. I doubted the stalker could know my private life, seeing as he disappeared before the drama happened yesterday, I was not worried. He must be some guy who happened to be there when I was.

Buzz, Buzz

I reached for my phone and realized it was Maisie's, I had left my phone in my bag downstairs, shit.

"YES!" She punched the air before turning her phone screen to me.

"NO SCHOOL TOMORROW!" She did a little dance on the bed jiggling back and forth. Did I forget to mention that Maisie hated school with a passion. She told me she was going to see Taylor tomorrow and called her dad to come pick her up. He arrived shortly and Maisie left. I sat on my bed looking at the note. Picking up and holding it in my hand I convinced myself it must be Brooke. I chucked the note out my window into the snow hoping it would destroy it.

I did not want to see that little ginger bitch again.

Chapter Eight

Robyn

After devoting a few hours last night making numerous calls to different restaurants I had snagged an interview at none other than; Bernie's. Getting a call back this morning not only woke me up extremely early, who would have guessed, but almost constructed the most perfect atmosphere for me to tumble down the stairs in order to retrieve my mobile phone. It had turned out that shortly after Maisie had left, I passed out on my bed as I was still in my clothes from yesterday. After forcing myself awake I put on my most alert voice to answer the call. A lady spoke, older by the sounds of it and she implied that she was interested in my CV and wondered if I could be round by four so the manager could interview me. After indulging in a small moment of victory I skipped back to my room I was disgusted with myself for having to peel out of clothes from yesterday. I threw them into the wooden washing basket which I had received for Christmas last year and hopped in the shower. Trying to fathom the events that took place yesterday I was disappointed to see no tea greeting me this morning. To be honest I was kind of hoping it would be a repetitive thing, but beggars can't be choosers.

After wrapping myself, and my hair, in a towel I evaluated the situation: I had a call from Bernie's, they wanted me in for an interview at four Pm, if that goes well, they want me to work tonight.

It was around seven by this point, I had made the choice to give myself extra time in the shower to refresh. Dad's car was gone again meaning that he had already left for work. A two-pound coin was lazing on my desk. It was the two pounds that the two old ladies had given us yesterday. I am glad there are people like that in this world but was still surprised she wanted us to buy an ice cream in this weather. Speaking of weather, most of the snow had disappeared now leaving just a thin crust surrounding the corners of streets, the letter that Brooke had left in my canvas was gone which could only mean my plan worked and it had dissolved successfully.

I was already planning my outfit, should I go basic or make a statement? Well, it was Bernie's so making a statement might be too much. I dug through my wardrobe but nothing seemed right at first glance, I even considered looking through my wash basket. I was desperate, digging through my basket I found nothing but a stained pain of jeans, socks and underwear. Since I had to bring my wash basket down earlier this week most of my clothes were back in my wardrobe. Eyeing up a pair of smart black trousers I paired them with a mustard jumper, I tucked in into the trousers and secured it with a mocha-brown belt. I looked like I had been pulled through a Pinterest board, however I did not mind, looking in the mirror I admired myself. I found my confidence had been growing the last few days and I guess that is due to the fact I was starting to realize what Dylan had done to me, it just clicked one day. That day I decided that I did not have to play by his rules anymore.

The time edging closer to four I hurried to the bus with my heart pounding in my chest.

Sitting watching the manager, twiddling my thumbs, he asked question after question. He was a tall man dressed in a white collared shirt and shiny shoes, almost as shiny as his head, he was a chubby man with a beer belly. He seemed to rarely smile but I believed I was doing well, having rehearsed on the bus, I felt confident. I was trying to put into practice what I had been taught in secondary school: make eye contact, sit straight, do not mumble. No pauses occurred in between his questions, I was worried he was not taking my answers in and my confidence started to drain. I wondered what life he leads at home whether he had a wife or kids? I have to admit working at Bernie's might not seem like the ideal job or career, although after going on research tangents with Maisie last night I found it paid well.

He finished off the evaluation, taking my final answer in this time, proceeding into the office he looked over his notepad which he had been scribbling illegible thoughts. Then looking back at me, I suddenly started to feel conscious about what I was wearing and rethinking all of my answers. Ten minutes stretched to twenty before he wandered back in with a uniform in his hands. It was not too bad of an outfit, could be worse.

"Good news, we'd like to offer you a position as waitress, as you spoke with my colleague on the phone this morning you'll be starting tonight, and your shift ends at nine. See me once your shifts end and I will give you your first pay. I have your phone number, so I will text your next dates we want you in, and all tips are given to me, and we share them out at the end of the month. Okay?" Yes! I nodded and gave a convincing yet 'not too much' smile. Taking the clothes and fist bumping the air once I was out of view. I slipped into the bathroom stall to change, he gave me a key to a small locker that we had to put our phones and belongings into. I tidied myself up in the mirror, he informed me to watch what other people were doing and to ask them if I had any questions and not to bother him as he would be busy taking calls and reservations.

Likewise, I spent the next few hours bringing out orders, around seven it started to get busy, I had never been to Bernie's at this time and was surprised at how many people came here to eat. Tables were filling up and shouting started coming from the kitchen. Orders were piling up, and we were bumping into each other nearly having a burn case on our hands. I eyed up Brooke almost falling through the door in ridiculously tall heels, she was dressed to impress and beside her stood another man. Not Dylan. It seemed Maisie's suspicions were right, god she moved on quickly, it has not even been forty-two hours yet. She glared at me and snarled as she waltzed past me to a booth in the corner. I had never really been to the back of Bernie's. It was illuminated by LED lights and signs, extremely different to the quiet coffee shop at the front. After almost getting slammed by the two-way door I had Brooke call me over by whistling, as if I were some sort of collie, irritable I walked over gripping my notepad and putting on a fake smile. "What can I do for you?" My anger seeped out. Ignoring my question, she said,

"I hope that little friend of yours is happy with herself, she humiliated me in front of everyone, did you know I got laughed at?" Brooke was pathetic, and the fact that no one cared she was there, or even noticed, made it even more humorous. I could tell she wanted me to snap and have a go at her, but I was not going to lose my job over her dramatizing her life to the point she thought she was the main character.

"Can I get another beer?" The guy sitting beside her said, breaking my eyes away from Brooke, I feasted my gaze upon one of the most gorgeous boys I had ever seen. He was perfectly sculpted and very tanned. His hair was black and frizzy but trimmed leaving a fade circling his head. The most amazing thing was his eyes, light green, he was studying me.

"Oh Yeah this is my new boyfriend by the way I upgraded, so sad you're still clinging onto Dylan like a lost puppy. You know when we were having sex, he said I was the best he'd ever had" She grinned from ear to ear pleased with herself and if that wasn't enough already, she laughed in my face. I have to admit that I was really embarrassed for her.

Her exceedingly-too-good to be true new boyfriend seemed to share the same opinion as he had now shuffled away from her and was gazing around the room, looking for anything he could pay attention to except her. Scribbling his order on a notepad

I told him I would be right back with his order. Whilst walking back to the bar I felt someone grab my arse cheek with an unfathomable grip. A Yelp left my mouth, like a puppy that had its tail stood on, I snapped my head around. An older man with a beer belly and a white beard grinned and raised his eyebrows. *Run Angel*. Listening to the voice I ran to the bar into the busiest parts of the restaurant not realizing I was hyperventilating the barmaid urged me to come to the back, abandoning her role, she patted me on the back before storming out the back and around the corner where I had run from. I could feel tears welling up in my eyes and streaming down my face.

Almost seconds later came shouting and with that the old man cursed his way out the front door, she came back to me with a warm smile and used a bobby pin that was clipped to her belt to return a strand of hair that had escaped from her low-lying ponytail held together in a black-fabric hair tie.

"Are you okay my love?" She spoke bringing me in for a hug and stroking my head. I had never caught her name. She was a Latino woman and smelt of honey. She made me feel safe even though I only met her a few hours ago. I was told to go to the bathroom to calm myself down. She gave me a few napkins from under the bar and ushered me through before turning back and continuing pouring drinks. I left my notepad on the side, and she informed me that she will get someone else to take care of it. She explained that he came in every weekend and there was always trouble, he came in at rush hours so he would not be thrown out, and he would hide behind corners or chairs to avoid staff. What a sad man. Walking into the disabled bathroom I locked the door and sat down on the lid of the toilet with my head in hands. I heard that voice again. My mind toyed like a cat playing with a ball of yarn. I could try and communicate, no one could get me in here I needed to see if it were in my head. I am probably just going crazy. I took a deep breath,

"Hello?"

Hi.

I panicked; I did not expect anyone to answer. I was going mental. Scrambling to my feet I looked in the mirror and splashed water on my face, a light knock came from the door, I froze.

"Sweetie? It is Martha. Are you okay in there?" No, I was not okay. You know what, it was just me hallucinating or something. Perhaps someone was smoking, and I breathed it in and made me think someone was talking, although I had no idea of how drugs worked, I managed to convince myself that was true. Putting on my 'I'm fine just a bit upset face' I walked out, Maria greeted me with a warm smile, she placed a hand softly on my back as she walked me out into the chaos of the diner.

"Are you sure you are okay?" I was not, not entirely. Pushing what had happened to the back of my mind I continued working. I gave her a smile and a nod then headed back out.

*

Stuffing a little brown packet that contained my wages into my pocket, I placed the clothes I had arrived in, into a small bag and headed home. Not wanting to wait for the bus I headed home on foot. It was nearly ten Pm and only a few streetlamps lit the ground I walked on. The snow had not settled and only specks remained.

Now that I was alone, with nothing to distract myself, I could not help my mind pulling up the event in the bathroom. It could not be possible. The thought of having someone in my head disturbed me, how were they doing it? They cannot. It is impossible. I was just imagining things…unless,

"Hello?" I took a chance and instantly regretted it.

A pregnant pause.

Um…hello?

Fear riddled through my consuming every muscle in my body, I crouched down for the fear of my fainting. My head felt too heavy, and I felt my body swaying side to side. I was almost certain I was going to pass out leaving me victim to the streets late at night.

Footsteps huddled towards me, getting heavier every second. I had an urge to run, clawing at the floor I tried to pull myself up, but I still feel weak.

Arms grabbed me around the waist and pulled me up. My body seized. This was it.

"Robyn! Robyn! Are you okay?" It was my dad. I flung myself at him hugging him as hard as I could. I felt safe. Furthermore, I wanted to go home, I needed to get out of here. It was cold and freezing.

"I'm okay, I think I just got light-headed and passed out."

"Oh, thank god!" He was crying, tears formed at the corners of his eyes, but he held them back not wanting me to see him distressed. He carried me to the car and helped me into the backseat. After closing the door, he ran round to the other side and hopped in. We sat in awkward silence while he got the engine running.

"How did you know I was there?" I questioned wanting to break the silence. It was almost unbearable. He was quick to answer,

"I was driving home from work when I saw you, so I pulled the car up and here we are." He was monotone before adding,

"Are you sure you're okay, we haven't spoken properly in a while, and I'm sorry I haven't been home its ju-"

"Listen dad it's fine honestly, I am just tired, and can we forget this happened? Please?" I interrupted. I did not want this to affect us and essentially, I did not feel like confessing about this 'magic man' voice I had been hearing. It was not fair, he had enough to deal with without me having problems.

"I'll call the school, and you can take the day off tomorrow. Just to make sure everything's in check." This was not a question; he was not going to let me if I begged him. So, I tried to bargain.

"What about if I go to the library tomorrow, get some studying in so I don't fall behind" I knew it was odd for me to want to work when most people pretend to be ill to get off school but frankly, I did not feel like sitting in bed all day.

"Alright." He responded. We settled in silence the rest of the journey home.

Once we got home, I went to the kitchen to make us a brew, a gesture to say sorry. Nothing felt real. I felt like I was in a fever dream, I was questioning whether I had heard that voice at all. Could it just be from not eating that much recently? No... I had been eating more over the last few days so that could not be true. Maybe if I just stay talking, I could get some answers? But if I tried to make contact it might open up some type of portal. Who knows, I have probably read too much sci-fi. I do not believe this was linked to the guy in the hoodie as he was not in the restaurant and I do not think I was followed there. Normally I have a sense if he is near, an unruly feeling but there was nothing. Maybe it was all in my head after all. Attempting not to burn my fingers on the sides of the cup I gently placed the cup down onto a coaster that sat on a small square table next to dad's chair. Upon looking up I found he had already fallen asleep, in the hope of him waking up, I left it there and plodded upstairs.

After peeling out of my work clothes and chucking them in my wash basket, due to them getting splashed with gravy which wouldn't have happened if someone hadn't have come through the wrong door, I got a call from Maisie.

"So how did it go!" She sounded enthusiastic, more than I was.

"Eh, I got groped by some guy, oh and did I mention Brooke was there with the most gorgeous man I had ever seen." I was not even going to try and cover it up at this point it was pretty terrible, awful in fact.

"Oh shit, I'm sorry girl."

"Wait. How did you know I was there? I never told you I got hired, or even a call back for that matter."

"Oh yeah, I was with Taylor, we walked past and saw you serving. We were going to come in, but it was too busy."

"Fair enough, anyway I'm going to get to bed Maisie, I'll see you whenever." I was not going to bed, but I did not feel like talking to people at the moment I gave her a civil laugh and ended the call.

I was not feeling particularly optimistic but instead of letting the evening go to waste I decided to start adding paint to my sketch. Having been painting for almost four hours, filling in the wings, background and most of the bodily features I finally, feeling tired enough to escape this nightmare and start a new, wrapped myself in the sheet, despite my recurring hopefulness, I had a hunch that tomorrow would be wrapped in a belt of sombre.

Chapter Nine

Robyn

A small paper note lay on my desk neatly folded and central.

Interest made me thirsty as I unfolded the note it read,

Hey! Sorry for scaring you yesterday, I really did not mean too and

that was not my intention. I thought you wanted to communicate once you said hi, but I guess you were not expecting me to answer. You are

not crazy I promise. I would introduce myself in person if I could, but

I am not allowed. My apologies. I wrote this note as it's a material

sign that you aren't crazy. I know this must be scary, but I promise I

am not here to hurt you. I am here to protect you, Angel.

-Murdoc x

It had been written in a watery biro pen that happened to be

missing from my pencil holder.

Right. So, this was real. There was a magical man or woman

now protecting me, guessing by the name it was more likely to

be a male and the voice yesterday had been deeper than a

veritable female. At least I was not crazy, unless I was

imagining this, what if there was no note at all and this was just

part of a dream? Sitting on the end of my bed with the note

clasped in my hand so hard it was starting to tear, my gaze fixed to the wall. If there were any ghosts floating around my room they would now be questioning if they were inconspicuous to the human eye. Could this possibly explain the man who was traveling behind me. That was the only explanation of course, it had to be him the one who was hiding in the trees and following me around the shopping centre. But the question dwelled of who he was. What was stopping him, surely not his mother or father? Maybe he was on house arrest? But how? That couldn't be, he wouldn't have been able to get into my house to leave the note. Oh, shit. He had been in my house, in my room! He was in my room last night, while I was none the wiser. I ran through all the times I had wished I had remembered to close my curtains whilst getting changed. Pinching my arm to prove I was not in a dream, I was almost thrillful that someone somewhere was looking out for me? But speculated how he knew me. It could not perchance be someone from school, no one knew where I lived, and most people had never showed any interest especially not to go to lengths to break into my house. Fumbling my phone out of my back pocket I urgently called Maisie to inform her of my discovery but hung up on the first ring remembering she is in class and would not be able to pick up till lunch. I deliberated whether I should maybe want to call the police but at the same time the chances of them believing my story would be next to nothing. I had no compelling evidence and I had disposed of the note.

Sticking to my claim to dad yesterday that I was going to the library I scanned over the items that I needed to take with me and placed them in my work bag then shortly headed out to the library.

A pleasant smile rose above the town beaming down, although there were no drastic changes of warmth in the air the winter sun still beamed. Shooting beams of light onto the ground guiding us to our destinations. Despite the 'summer smiles' the trees were stripped of clothing forcing us to realize the reality that Christmas was coming. The wind had a bite to it nipping at your face with its sharp teeth, it tangled my hair round my face and as a result I clipped it into place with a small metal clip that I always kept on my belt.

Streets were busy today; people were politely walking out of banks and barbers. The local bakers were shouting their deals of the day with tremendous ambition. Kids hung onto coats heading for a forced 'day out', clinging onto their mum's coats and bags that carried the essentials for the day. Others were screaming and kicking on the floor having parents curse them to be quiet, coincidentally right outside Arthur's Toy Box. It used to be my favourite place dad would take me birthday shopping, he would give me the money that my uncles and aunties had sent in birthday cards and let me spend it on whatever I wanted. He believed kids should be able to spend their own money on what they desired, within reason of course, I remember on my twelfth birthday I purchased my first proper art easel that still sits in my room to this day. Neighbour- like smiles circled the streets, crossing over roads and jumping into the most unexpected people. Three teenage boys and two girls with all assortment of hair colours sped round the corners on skateboards, swerving cars, and off down the hill.

I entered a crowd of people, pushing my way through, I repeatedly said "sorry" not like they could hear me over the market callers and the rumbling of cars. A man, slightly taller than me, walked past. He accidently brushed my shoulder a little too hard. I stumbled back, in the sea of people I reached out my hand, in the severity and possibility that I could fall backwards into the road, his eyes locked onto mine.

I flung backwards, everything became a blur as the wind popped my ears and hair disorientated my view. Screams came from the roads and brakes screeched.

I was going to die.

The sounds of engines drummed closer, became greater. I slammed my eyes closed preparing for the impact; Everything went black.

I was in shadow with only small beams of light piercing through the darkness. I thought of Maisie and of dad, I thought of mum. I thought of us watching Friday night telly with dinner on our laps laughing at the TV and pointing at the blatent stupidity of some characters' decisions. Dad had spilt gravy down his shirt that night and was running to the kitchen to wash it off before mum saw. I thought of going to a club that seemed like so many years ago with Maisie and then having to hold her hair while she threw up in the toilet. The stomping of feet radiated in the background in beat with the thudding of the music. It is so silent now.

Vehicles shrieked from a distance. Distraught shouting and gasping filled my ears, bringing me back to my senses. A metallic residue filled my mouth and boiled my throat. Opening my eyes to see the road in front of me, I was crowded in a circle of people, I was slumped backwards having to peer through their legs and my neck twinged in pain from any movement, my ears were ringing everything seemed to zoom in and out rapidly.

"I've got an ambulance on the phone; they'll be here in a minute!" A female voice bawled from outside the circle.

"What was that?" Another man canvassed. He seemed closer and sat on my right. I cracked my head up ignoring the multiple popping sounds my neck produced. Almost as if there was an echo, another man nodded and then repeated the previous question. He was looking to the sky and then back to me baffled. Gripping the nearest flower box, I attempted to haul myself up using the wooden ledge. My fingers dug into the soil coating my hands and filled the underside of my nails. The same woman that had been on the phone to the ambulance sat beside me and ushered me back to the ground and repeatedly told me it would all be okay. Fixing my gaze between the legs of the people huddled around me, I could see cars stopped at different angles and people were getting out and running over. Drivers were shouting at each other arguing over whose fault it was but then saying there was no damage to either of the cars. The baker had now stopped yelling and was standing on chairs outside his bakery to look at what had happened. People were whispering amongst each other and sirens were heard in the distance bearing closer with every blink of an eye. The lady that sat beside me smiled and a tear fell from her eye to my hand.

"They're coming now!" she proclaimed.

Kids were now crying as sirens pierced ears. And an ambulance and a police car messily parked on the side of the road and ran over to me. With the muchness of it all I started to feel my head getting heavy and my eyes drooping,

"It's okay you're in safe hands now, can you tell me what happened?" A female voice asked, she was impressively calm, but I suppose that is from being in a job like this.

I think I got hit, I'm not sure." I spurted. My head started to feel dizzy and the embarrassment of it all made it worse. I hated the feeling of all eyes being on me. I wanted to start this day over to be back in the safe comfort of the sheets.

"It's okay, we're going to take care of you. We are taking you to the hospital. The police will take care of the cause they'll come to the hospital to question you when you're stable."

Feeling myself slide into unconsciousness I crossed my fingers. Please let me be okay.

*

White lights swarmed my vision. I had recollection of being in a vehicle, most probably the ambulance. Everything was now still. Apart from an aching pain in my neck and back I looked up to see a small light hanging above my head swinging ever so slightly hinting to the fact it had been recently disturbed. The constant clicking of machines and clutter of footsteps grounded me, the room smelt of hand sanitizer, it burned my nose and made my eyes swell. Focusing my gaze downwards I saw a white sheet covering my body. It was thin, leaving me a tad chilly. Looking to my right I spotted my docs sitting awkwardly next to an armchair that was occupied by my dad. Noticing my consciousness, he rushed over with a smile and hugged me awkwardly. Warmth seeped into my cheeks. It had been over a minute now he was not letting go. Candidly, I didn't want him too.

"I heard about what happened. I'm so glad you are okay!" I felt a tear land on my nose and rush to my cheek. He stood back up and wiped his eyes, his smile beaming. Placing his glasses on his nose he stumbled back to the chair he had claimed his own, puffy red skin surrounded his eyes showing he had been crying earlier. Realizing he had come back from work for me, planted a seed of guilt in my stomach as his boss was not the nicest. The clicking of shoes came round the corner, a tall woman with a pixie cut and medium brown skin held a clipboard with multiple pieces of paper flipped over the opposite way. She gave me a warming smile exposing her almost too white teeth. A single nose ring looped through her nose and complimented her eyebrows that had been freshly shaped and tinted in a darker brown almost mud-coloured.

"Robyn is it?" She checked with an comforting smile that a grandma would have. I nodded with confirmation, she glanced at her clipboard again and followed it with her pen before meeting my eyes again.

"So, from earlier scans you have no vital injuries, a few bruises on the lower back and spine but apart from that you do seem to be unharmed," I gave a sigh of relief.

"However, there are signs of malnourishment. You are quite a bit underweight." she twisted her face into a concerned glare.

I should have known that was coming although I had been getting better with my eating habits my body did not yet reflect that.

She explains to dad that I may need to be referred to a therapist in eating behaviours, and we do have services free on the NHS that are available. My phone was placed next to me and I randomly scrolled through the home screen while they discussed times and appointments that are going to be quickest to get me into. The whole-time dad had this look of pain in his eyes, a desperation to be better. I knew he believed he was not that good of a dad. I wanted nothing more than to go and give him the biggest hug and confront him. It was not his fault; nothing was his fault. How could it be? He was doing his best at work to provide for us, he was the reason I had food in the fridge and a roof over my head. The smile he had once worn faded as he was now met with the future that if my eating habits continued like this then I would be back here again this time being force-fed.

Dad got on the phone while I was given a small meal I was required to eat before I went home, I had no trouble, and I was rather quite hungry. The jelly tasted more like rhubarb than strawberry. On the other hand, the crackers were nicely salted, not as stale as I expected.

Interrupting dads and the Nurses conversation, two policemen walked in. They were dressed sharply in uniform and had a notepad in hand. They walked over to me and read the sign at the end of my bed that had my name, age and height and possibly my cause for being here written down. The broad men looked at each other rather than at me. Both were dressed in black and had clean-cut stubble sat round their chin they did seem to be good friends from the banter they had on the way in.

"Are you Robyn Skinner?" The cop on the left asked.

"Yes." I had not had many interactions with the police, but I was nervous. Dad walked over and shook their hands and explained that he was my father, they told him that they were just doing some questioning and that they should not be here long. They had a tone of sarcasm in their voice as if dad had asked if they were stupid for not realizing it already.

"Were going to ask you a series of questions about the events that happened earlier today, is that okay?"

"Mhm."

"So how did you get into the road?"

"I believe I must've lost my balance in this crowd I was in; I think I grabbed onto someone but then fell back."

"Okay and do you recall how you got to the other side of the road?" He raised an eyebrow.

"No, it was a blur, I fell into the road then I was in darkness, which was when I got hit, and then I must've been thrown to the other side of the road."

"You didn't get hit Robyn." The nurse corrected from the other side of the room. Then how did I get there, why was I thrown into complete darkness?

"Right, so how did you get here if you weren't hit?" The cop raised his voice and he sounded like I was wasting his time.

"I- I believe I was in an ambulance. Someone rang saying there was an accident, so I anticipated that I had got hit, but the results came back saying I was unharmed…" I stopped talking as I know what I had been saying made no sense and I looked as though I was committing a stunt.

*

With the double doors flaring open with an expansive entrance and impeccable drama Maisie ploughs into the room.

"OMG ROBYN! I heard! Are you okay? I am so sorry I did not answer your call. What happened?" She exclaimed, changing all the attention in the room to us. Dad scratched his forehead and followed his brow down his nose and caressed it.

"I'm okay Maisie really I'm fine," I was delighted to see her. She was good old Maisie, it appeared as though she had left school early to come see me which I guess was a good thing for her. She seated by my side whilst the nurse was addressing my dad about me coming back for more checks to make sure I was not experiencing any other troubles. I perceived something in the window. A bird but huskier, I blinked, but then vanished from sight.

Maisie enquired with my dad if I could spend the night at hers and dad consented reluctantly. I could not pick fault with him. I had a lack of knowledge of the course I might be put on and how long I would have to be on it, but the nurse said it would be advisable. I had gone to therapy before, but it was at school instead. It was after my mum's death that I attended for months, personally I think they were not that good at the consoling part but I guessed they helped, having said that I personally feel like a part of me is missing. A nothingness that is a mystery of how to fill.

I was discharged not that long after, with a new date we had to adhere to, to return and check up on my progress. We arrived at Maisie's and I gave dad a small hug and kiss on the cheek. After she told me about Dr Outen's humorous lessons she enquired about how the events took place today, she had been told briefly in the hospital but wanted to hear the whole story from my point of view and version of events.

"So, what happened?" She appeared distressed almost as if she were steadying herself for the news she could receive, she knew I was okay, but something hid behind her eyes.

"I was just walking to the library and I bumped into this man, and then next thing I knew I was in darkness, then I was on the other side of the road" I cognized what I was saying did not make sense, but it was all I knew myself. I was still convinced I got hit. I must have at least collided with something or was it just my brain taking me to somewhere nicer, that brief few seconds where I was in the comfort of my living room, in the club with Maisie. The moment I was cast into that shadow I weighed in that I had a want, a passion uncovered in my chest greater than I had ever felt before.

"Damn, what about the bird?" She asked, looking like I knew what she was talking about.

"The bird? What does a bird have to do with this?" I enquired. I cannot tell whether she was making a joke about me getting to the other side of the road or if she was being serious.

"Yeah, it's been on everyone's Facebook that when you got 'hit' it was like a shadow flew across the road overshadowing you and then went to the sky, people found feathers on the road." Maisie forcibly pulled her phone out of her pocket and proved her statement by pointing out multiple videos that had filmed the aftermath of the accident for whatever reason. Majority were tourist videos or selfies with a shadow airborne in the background. I marvelled if the same bird-like figure I saw through the hospital window was linked to the bird feathers that had been on the floor after the accident.

*

The sky was now as black as school shoes, an owl was hooting in the distance too far away to see but just close enough to hear its song. LEDs wedged to the wall above her bed filled the room with a purple gradience. It changed the colours of Maisie's posters making you think you were on an acid trip.

Maisie was asleep next to me snoring, it was something she always criticizes everyone else for doing yet she was the main cause. Thinking back to the note I received earlier I established that I did not want to play a game with this magic man anymore. Whether he had noticed it or not he was scaring the shit out of me recently, the watching, frequent tapping into my head and not to mention the breaking into my house. I scowled at the thought of him seeing me vulnerable. Despite all this something made me want to talk to him. I wanted to know his life and how he had the ability to talk to me through my mind. It was remarkable really.

"Hello? Are you there?" I blurted my whole torso constricted for the outcome.

A pregnant pause.

Is this another test?

"No, it's not, I want answers" my breath accelerated.

Well, it is late, so I think you should get to sleep.

"What? I almost died today, and I don't want to play games."

You did not die because I got you out of the way.

"…what?" So, it was true then, something had got me out the way. Before he could answer I asked,

"So, your Murdoc? The one who left the note? The one who's been in the trees."

Yeah, that is right. I am the guy in the trees. There was an essence of sarcasm in his voice, as if he were mocking me for not solving this mystery earlier. I could feel him grinning at his remark.

"Why is this happening? Why are you in my head?"

Look it is late and been a long day Angel and I will explain it all another time just let us get some sleep.

"Angel?"

It is a nickname. Do you not like it?

I spoke too quickly for my own good,

"no, no I do like it, but this is the first time I've actually spoken

to you so isn't it weird?"

Not if you do not make it weird, now get some sleep.

"Goodnight then?" He was right. I could barely keep my eyes

open let alone sit and listen to him explain everything, as much

as I wanted to know it would have to wait.

Goodnight Angel.

Chapter Ten

Robyn

"So, can you tell me why you're here? I've had a brief report from the hospital, but I need to know your reason!" She had her hands intertwined with each other on the desk and one golden ring sat on her fourth finger of her left hand. Black coffee had stained her teeth and the sheer quantity that she must drink had made the room smell bitter. Besides that, the vintage furnishing gave the room a cosy vibe, not too much like a grandma's house but just that touch of maturity like a nice wine instead of WKD.

"I had a problem with my eating, but I am getting better, I've been eating more to a vast extent and on a regular basis. I'm just here because my dad said I have to go." The chairs were abnormally high leaving me swinging my legs under the chair. She looked me up and down,

"Yeah, I'm sure you are, so we're just going to run through this questionnaire, and then we'll give you your care plan!" Her glasses were placed so far down her nose she had to look down to see through them, she was filing papers and making a fish face as she did so.

The questions were fairly simple until she asked if I'd had any sort of therapy here before. She had already known I had therapy before as it was written down in my application, although it was not with this organization, they organized it a lot differently. Now withstanding the fact, she had already been told about my past by my dad but she was persistent for me to tell it again, to pull back the emotions that I had not touched for so many years. What was the need, moving on with my life was hard enough without tapping into the memories again? I had not thought about that morning for so long how it had been lost in time, I put the events together. They clawed their way up my spine with their shrivelled and decaying hands that looked as if they had been pulled and crimped in the years of youth.

She looked at me, depressing her head again, and handed me a tissue pinching it between her ruby-red nails. I dabbed my eyes trying not to smudge any mascara that might have escaped in the process. I hated her for making me remember. As a professional surely, she should know that my mother's tragedy was not for here, we were here to talk about my weight. I maneuvered the conversation back by telling her what I normally eat in a day. Despite the tension we had created, she agreed with me on my favourite choice of tea.

*

Although it was only five pm Bernie's was packed, I guess there was something going on tonight a special event maybe or perhaps a birthday? Balloons circled the walls making it almost impossible to get through the crowd without your ears getting raped by screeching of the balloons. I signalled Martha who was loading cups into the dishwasher under the bar. She was grinning from ear to ear, she was a smile herself. She migrated to the kitchen signalling plates that were becoming stacked up, I rushed over, checked the tickets and then headed back out to the chaos that was the main floor. A sea of hairlines formed my view. The plate was riskily balancing on the palms of my

173

fingers above my head. With the heat in the room rising around me a driblet of sweat traced my forehead, the heat of bodies in the room plus the potent smell of BO and perfumes was making me feel sick. Working my way to a table at the back became easier as people used this space as more of a lounge, black sofas were placed in the corners and only a few tables sat here. Sitting at a table was none other than Maisie and what seemed to be Taylor, I wished she would have told me she was going to be here. Taylor was prettier than she looked in her pictures. She had chocolate-brown skin that was powdered in gold dust and had splashes of freckles on her face. Sitting below her shoulders black box braids were done to perfection in neat rows with no wisps appearing. I understood now what Maisie had found so engrossing about her. Despite her amazing features I desperately wanted to know how her eyeliner was that sharp, and how she got the lines on her lipstick so clean.

With a smile appearing on her face Maisie had either spotted me or the food she stood up and took the plates right out of my hand. I gave an eye roll, classic.

"So, nice to see you again! Oh! And this is Taylor who I've been talking about." She treated me like we had not seen each other for years when the reality was, we saw each other only this morning. She faced Taylor and blew her a kiss making me cringe slightly. Well, if they are happy that is all that matters really. Standing up Taylor revealed her neon green strappy top with trippy pants and spiked platforms. She looked stunning and like she could curb stomp someone without any effort put in at all. She held out her hand that was bedazzled with bracelets and bangles, shaking her hand politely it was hard ignoring the cold tinge of the gold and obscure rings that sat on her fingers. I traced one of them to be in the shape of a frog and sat next to it a gold snake that twirled round her finger.

"Nice to meet you Robyn, Maisie here won't stop talking about you so it's finally nice to put a face to a name." She shot Maisie a look and so did I.

"Yeah, same here! I wish you could see how excited she gets when she talks about you." Ha! Sweet revenge, Maisie held her head in her hands embarrassed. Maisie did put on this 'hard' persona but really, she was as much as a softie as me. I could see them together, Maisie had spoken to me earlier in the week that she had been looking at adoption websites, although Maisie had never spoken to me about having children before, she seemed surprisingly fixed on the idea that her and Taylor would be having children at some point. With Maisie making a sign to Taylor that she wanted to speak with me for a few minutes Taylor nodded and winked at her and headed off to the bathroom signalling for me and Maisie to talk in private for a few minutes. I figured I like this girl; she was polite and seemed to be down to Earth unlike Maisie's other girlfriends. One of Maisie's past relationships consisted of her valuables getting burnt if she did anything that she 'wasn't supposed to'. Another Maisie had been a woman that had the radical belief that aliens existed and would spend hours on the roof waiting for them to give her a 'sign' what that sign remained a mystery to us as she did not seem to know herself.

"So, I had that therapy session today,"

"Oh yeah how was it?" She took a sip of her drink and ended up dribbling most of it down herself.

"Tragic, she kept bringing up therapy with my mum and avoided most questions of food, which was the main reason why I was there so why deflect the questions." A lump in my throat started to swell leaving me choked up and my eyes turned glassy.

"Oh, I'm sorry Robyn, she's an old bint, remember that okay. That was well out of order." She hugged me and then kissed my forehead gently before returning to her seat. Even though Maisie had never met the woman we shared the same opinion. Taylor had returned now; I was being called back to the kitchen. Despite the fact Maisie had almost finished her food I told her to enjoy her meal and hoped she and Taylor would have fun. She shot me a thumbs up before I returned through the crowd back to the kitchen. Dad gave me a ring checking up on me, although he was at work, he had now found time, he asked how work was going and that he was so proud of me for getting a job and being able to recover this quickly. I would be getting off soon allowing me to finally talk to Murdoc again. Not only did the thought get me curious but it also got me excited. Something about me wanted to talk to him. I wanted to hear his voice ringing in my head. Although this time I knew

I did not have to be scared, he was protecting me. And if that was the truth then why?

*

With the warmth of the teacup soaking through my hands, I carried on up the stairs trying my best not to spill it as I had accidentally poured too much in the cup and the tea was now only a few millimetres away from the top. After settling the tea down on my nightstand, I peeled out of my work clothes and chucked them back in the wash as they now reeked of beer and weed. Someone must have been smoking tonight, if not the whole restaurant. My whole body felt dirty like the top layer of oil on a broth leading me to the shower.

Wrapped in a fluffy towel I eyed up the painting that I had not yet finished. Not only had I missed two days of school I was now falling behind on the only hobby I have, well if you could

179

count drinking tea as a hobby then I do in fact have two hobbies.

I Sat in bed scrolling through Instagram and sipping my tea letting it savour in my mouth for a few minutes before gliding down me through like liquid honey. The news was buzzing with my accident yesterday and already several videos had popped up on YouTube discussing the shadowy figure that seemed to carry me across the road. I suppose I could officially call myself an internet sensation however I had not been asked to appear on any conspiracy podcasts yet.

Hairs erected on my back in alertness, someone was here, questionably I was not scared.

You looked pretty today.

"I was crying in the Therapy room, and don't sneak up on me like that."

Well, it is kind of hard to warn you, can't really tap you on the shoulder, can I? Anyway, back to the point; you looked pretty today. Gorgeous in fact.

"I'm starting to think you're stalking me now."

Not stalking just…protecting.

"Why?"

Why what?

"Why are you so protective, you've never met me."

Because it is what we do when we meet our person, we protect them with everything we have.

"Our person? Whose we? Who are you talking about?"

Well, truth is I am not human as such I-

"Are you a vampire!?"

No.

"Werewolf?!"

Nope.

"Don't tell me! Hmm… Merman?"

EW no.

"Just asking."

Look, I am not anything you have heard of.

A rumble of the L200 pulled up then the doors opened, just on cue he shouted me down.

I believe your dad's back

"Yes, I'm aware."

We will Speak later if you can Angel.

Bringing in two mugs of tea dad kicked off his shoes and gave me a kiss on the head. He sipped his tea and clicked his tongue in satisfaction. I pondered if I should tell him about Murdoc? It would not go down well but something about Murdoc made me want to sit and talk for hours, he made me want to stay up late at night, I wanted to be close to him.

"I have some news and I wanted to discuss it with you first before I make any final decisions." He expressed. I already knew it was something to do with work and was worried he would be getting the sack. I mean, after he took abrupt times off work it does not matter the reason, his boss would not like it. His boss ran a strict company that would always need people there, well that is what dad was told however, the boss himself took multiple holidays every year with his family to some of the most amazing places in the world. I could not recall the last time I had been on holiday; I am pretty sure I have never left England, maybe as a child but certainly not a teenager or young adult. Maisie and I have been planning as young girls but it was hard for us to both contribute equal money as she found it hard to get employment.

"I've been asked to go on another business trip, a few weeks if that, I don't want to leave you alone, after all that's happened,

I'd feel like the worst dad in the world. But it's a big opportunity and could get me a promotion."

"Go, there's no question about it. I'll help you pack!" I understood that dad wanted to take care of me, I would have been the same in his situation but if he had a chance to improve both of our lives, he should take the chance. I questioned the accountability of the promotion as his boss refused to give bonuses even in the festive seasons. He followed me upstairs where I retrieved two suitcases from under his bed and started filing through his wardrobe for all his essentials. There was not much to choose from, dad seemed to have the biggest collection of brown trousers I had ever seen.

Half an hour later we were done, he had a taxi waiting outside as he gave me a kiss on the cheek and told me he would ring me when he got to Wales. Now alone I suppose most people would have a party with their new-found freedom, maybe a meetup or trash the house however I went right back to the kitchen to make another brew. He had left me just under three hundred pounds for food and transport and told me he put more credit on my phone, so I could ring him if I needed to. The house now felt cold, there was nothing to come home for now, dad had gone away before, but this time it felt different. Walking back through the hall I saw mum's picture, she was beautiful. Coco-brown hair curled down her back, she had natural springs in her hair that most people pay to get. Thankfully, she left them to me. She had grey eyes that held a chocolate brown centre, she was soft but independent. The picture was taken at my sixteenth birthday party, we had gone to a restaurant and dad thought mum looked so pretty he had to take a photo and get it printed out. He got a royal gold frame that contrasted nicely with the dark grey walls that lined the house. We had a scheme in mind but gave up once dad messed up the furniture and curtains. I thought mum would go mental but instead she decided to give up the idea of having a 'Pinterest worthy' house. We ended up with quite a dark house filled with plants in white pots that sat on wonky spruce shelves, dad insisted we did not need to waste money on someone else to put them up. We had not catered to the plants, other than watering, so they had grown down to the floor making it look almost like a greenhouse.

Shimmying up the stairs, setting down my tea and jumping into my bed I called out for Murdoc. There was no reply. I suppose he must have been busy or fallen asleep. I have to give it to him; it was almost one in the morning.

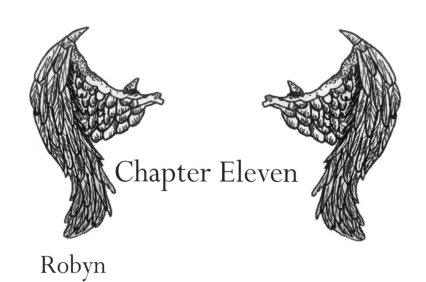

Chapter Eleven

Robyn

I sent a text to Dylan finally facing the promise I had made to

Maisie. I was going to do it tonight, whatever happened leaving

him would be my best shot at succeeding and taking back

control of my life. He took a few hours to respond, I had told

him to come round my house tonight as we needed to talk.

With my dad out I knew he would accept straight away. It was sad really. I felt sorry for him. He could get any girl he wanted but has created such a bad reputation for himself that no matter how much he would try to change it, if he ever had the desire too, he could not. They would not stay with him unless they were extremely desperate, but I do not believe anyone has low enough standers.

I had been working on the painting this morning adding the fine details, I still have not heard anything from Murdoc. I suppose he was busy. I still did not know what he was and the idea that he was not human excited me. I am not weird in that way. Just the fact that there are other paranormal and mythical creatures that were only in kids' books was remarkable. I longed to tell Maisie but was worried she would not believe me and even if she did, I had no proof, I had been talking to someone in my head who claims they are not human and would get me thrown in a psych ward before I could explain. So, it was our secret. He used 'we', so did that mean there were more of them? Did he have a family, if he could not see me then surely there must be some rules or boundaries he had to follow.

I had a few hours to spare before I had to take a day shift at work. Opening my art draw a single black feather lay at the back of the draw under a notebook, this had been the raven feather I had kept using on a future piece, something about it felt like it needed protecting. Could this be Murdoc's? If it was then it made sense for the size to stretch abnormally longer than a normal bird. It was rough in my hands but at the same time soft like mink fur.

What have you got there?

I shricked dropping the feather, it plummeted to the ground defying the term 'light as a feather'.

"I told you to stop scaring me!" My curtains were open. I peered out but could not see anything, or anyone for that matter. Bins rattled over the road, only a cat appeared chasing another down the road.

Like I said I do not mean to, so you got a big date tonight?

"More like I'm breaking up with him. Wait. How did you know I had texted him? Or who he is for that matter."

I know more than you think Angel.

"Fair enough."

Listen, I am not going to be here tonight I have got some stuff I need to sort out so be safe, just do not get yourself hurt.

So, he knew Dylan was unsafe. This was the point where I thought he must have been watching me for at least a few days or weeks for that matter. He sounded genuinely concerned about my safety. Although he had still not told me what he was I knew he had wings so I was guessing some sort of birdman?

Maybe a centaur. But I was not sure if centaurs had wings. If 'non-humans' were real, then sure enough there could be other creatures out of there.

"I'll try, Dylan's unpredictable to say the least."

No shit. I must get going, please stay safe for me.

"For you?"

Silence responded in his favour.

Chapter Twelve

Murdoc

The kingdom of Enlarnoc looked as bright as ever. It had been in peace for a millennium, ruled by king Ragnus. He was a warrior, pure pedigree. Although he was one of the most superhuman angels known to the earth as we know it, he had guards lining all doors and sides of the kingdom. The kingdom sat on top of a mountain with the towns below, floating on water the kingdom was the main trader of fish and water potions, the springs were nearby close to the woods, but the main towns and villages sat below the kingdom. Like any other cities you had the rich and the poor, some people were grouped together in suites with metal roofs, others were in hollowed out trees turning back to the traditional sleep patterns. The higher classes were in wooden buildings lit by candles. But the royals lived in the castle overlooking everyone either with disgust or desperation. A desperation to help those in need, although they did not need to eat regularly, they did need to consume something in order to survive. I walked up the mount of stairs with my wings trailing behind me. I remember climbing these stairs with Elliot. Plotting our escape and revenge on the king, we were threatened with being banished if we ever tried to get into the kingdom again. However, that was five years ago, and my growth spurt would hopefully make sure I got past the guards. They had horns at the apex of their wings sharpened into sharp spines and the horns that grew out of their head were sharpened to perfection by the blacksmiths. The castle came into view and looked as if it had been pulled from a children's storybook, their idea where dragons guarded and princesses that have been cursed lay. All stone was handled to perfection, every engraving or patterns chiselled into the stone held a story. The kingdom had stood here longer than anyone in our time, they say it was found by ancient warriors that built it up from the water creating a labyrinth of tunnels underneath, the kingdom supposedly held priceless artefacts. It was passed down for generations until today where it sat in the hands of Ragnus. I stood upon the drawbridge that connected to the great stone arch that rose high above the towns below. The kingdom had circle towers placed randomly up the hill, it was once used for defence against other kingdoms but since making peace thousands of years ago they had been deserted and were mostly used for storage or guards' sleeping quarters. The guards stood on sentry, walking across the drawbridge and under the portcullis I gazed above my head, I felt my stomach drop as there was no going back now. The guards had spotted me, they were walking over.

"Name?" One instructed, his eyes were burning into mine.

"Murdoc." They gave a laugh.

"The half boy! God your little stunt yesterday had all the boys laughing so thank you for that." I rolled my eyes. They were bending over to laugh as if someone had slipped, and they found it the funniest thing in the world.

"I was instructed to see the king." I said over their bellyful laugh. They turned still choking on their own humour and instructed me into the castle. The walls were just how I remembered them; grand, too high to touch the ceiling even if you jumped. We traversed up multiple stairs, it was deemed rude to fly indoors, an old wife's tale if that. Another flight of stairs later, we had arrived at two colossal double doors that almost took up the size of the wall.

As the great double doors swung open a shadow stepped into the light beaming in from the stained-glass windows and found himself to be more legend than man. The people had seen him in good times and in bad. He was built upon legs, dressed in silver armour with a black cape shredded to the back of his calves. His hair was long and up in a ponytail leaving the sides of his head shaved. Some sort of animal skull lay upon his head like a crown. He had intended to wear this skull as much as possible whether it be sentimental or simply for intimidation purposes. It was said that he wore the skull into battle with other kingdoms before making peace, and we won the wars of course. His face was marvellous, his cheeks look pinched. How

I loathed him. Various scars traced his face and scored down his neck to his heart that was ragged and dark brown. Tremendous wings filled his back that were so heavy with muscle that his posture leant slightly back when he walked. A permanent limp occurred in his leg. I was pushed through the doors hearing them slam behind me. This was my cue to face him, the man who had torn my family apart and could tear me to pieces if he pleased. His eyes locked with mine, they were full of untold pain, his brow retired over his eyes shielding them from his people. He never went out like he used to, he would fly around the kingdom delivering food to the people, he would open the kingdom and have parties to celebrate our freedom. Their kind. Now he locks himself in this kingdom only meeting for emergencies with no Queen by his side anymore he is believed to be dead by many.

"I didn't think I'd have to see you again. But here we are." His voice was raspy and gave a small chuckle at his own sarcasm. I was hesitant to say anything, I did not know what I could say. 'Sorry' did not seem appropriate and more like I was taking the mick.

"I've met her." I blurted. I was going to get banished anyway so might as well make my mark.

"And? Good for you lad." He smiled but then it quickly faded. I did not get to finish before he abruptly added,

"What's the problem then? Is she not good enough for you?" he sneered.

"No of course not-"

"Her wings are too small?"

"No, she's-"

"A healer?"

"NO. She's human." I'd had enough of his sarcasm, I desired to wipe the stupid smirk right off his ugly mug. The room fell silent. He marched over his hands curled into fists, he stopped only a few centimetres away from me. I could smell the hot breath breathing down on me, he believed I was scum, scum to the Earth and scum to Enlarnoc. There was no question about that.

"You know the rules. There is to be no mixing of humans and… your kind." He looked me up and down and centred his gaze back to my eyes attempting to frighten me into following this rule.

"She needs help."

"Well, I'll try and get her on the waiting list for a guardian angel." He said backing off.

"I know I can protect her." I informed. Flaring my wings, as a sign of dominance.

"But what about us? What about Enlarnoc! Your little stunt was all over the news!" I could not believe the nerve of this guy. Why should I care if they have never done anything for me? They took away my parents and killed my mother.

"She was going to die!" I was shouting now; my wings were fully outstretched now. He knew what he was doing; he had no look of remorse in his gaze.

"Then let her! She is of no use to us. You'll have to move on, or do you want us to take care of her, so you can match with someone you know."

"Are you insane? You're going to kill her?!" Who the fuck did he think he was? I wanted to pounce, to rip his guts out, to hang him from his own castle.

"I won't if you stay away from her." He sat on his throne and took a bite out of an apple and took a swig of what I thought to be Mugwort tea.

"But the humans won't know if I keep my wings hidden, I can do that if you haven't forgotten." I lowered my wings initiating what I wanted was to debate and not fight. I need to keep calm if we were to make any sort of agreement.

"I said no Murdoc."

"Why can't we mix?"

"Don't let the same thing that happened to your father happen to you. leave." He turned and whistled signalling his guards to come in to get me.

"TELL ME!"

"I SAID LEAVE!"

Two guardians gripped me under my arms and dragged me down the stairs. I was kicking trying to free myself from their grip. I was discarded down the stairs thrown through the front doors where I was blinded by the daylight. Any remorse I had for him or respect was now lost.

Dragging my feet down the main road of the village I kicked over some bins and smashed some nearby plant pots, I had no respect for this town. Enlarnoc had done nothing but hurt me and my family.

A Small tapping radiated on my shoulder, I spun round to be greeted with one of the elderly healers. Her wings were a dark brown, showing no signs of drug use. Rare but I suppose in her time of life she had experienced everything there was. She smiled as if I were an old friend.

"What's happened?" She was a lot shorter than me and had one eye blue whilst the other was green. It was not irregular for healers, although it was still amazing when it occurred. I explained to her that I had just been talking to the king, he was being unreasonable.

"Cut him some slack you know what he's been through." I blankly stared at her. She gave a worried smile noticing that I was not informed in this region.

"I think you should come inside." She led me back to her home. It was a wooden hut not that far from the main village, it resembles the shape of a toadstool. Inside was comforting and bigger than what you would imagine, the walls did not bend and had great windows letting loads of light in. Sitting on the main room was a fire burning. Whilst I was scrolling through her selection of old books, she poured two cups of tea. I returned to sit on one of the two chars she sat in front of me in a small armchair and sipped her tea gently.

"A long time ago, before you were born, Ragnus was a joyous king." she started.

"Yeah, I've heard that much." I sipped my tea and smiled.

"He had a daughter, a daughter called Lucy." I was taken back; I had never thought of him as a dad.

"She was an angel obviously and had fallen in love with a human. She was beautiful. Blonde with brown eyes and a smile that could have lit up a cave. She was head over heels for this boy, he was everything to her. Ragnus did not like it as all dad's wouldn't. But he allowed her to travel to the human villages to see him. One night she begged to be able to sleep over at his, to spend a night in the human villages. She did not come home...so he sought for her. He risked getting hunted and shot down, he risked the exposure of his men. The search went on for a few days until one of his men uncovered a body in a field. It was lucky none of them got hurt or shot down in the process. Her wings had been sawn off, and she had bled out, dragged and then dumped." A tear slipped from her eye,

"I remember when he came back, he had a private funeral, the next day he made the law to protect his people." She wiped her nose and sniffled. I had my mouth executing open. I did not realize I was crying until a tear dropped into my tea that splashed back to my hand. I wiped my eyes with the back of my hand and then smeared it on my trousers.

"I was friends with your mum, she'd come round for tea most of the time and when she went back to the human villages, she would drop you and Elliot at my house here."

"Thank you for telling me this, really. What should I do? My soulmate is human, we've never met, but she needs help." I spoke, my voice broken. She placed a hand on my leg, her eyes had gone red from crying.

"You need to do what's right for you. Lucy did not have a choice. You can appear human; you have the power to hide your wings. You have a shot as that life. So, take it, your mum would have wanted that. She said to me that she did not want you to grow up in a place that resented you, a place that made you have to hide. Go after her, leave here and do not look back. If they do not want you here then why follow their rules? Just be careful Murdoc." She gave me a heartful smile. I thanked her for the tea and made my way to the tree, Elliot had to come with me. If we were leaving, he was coming with me just like we planned all those years ago.

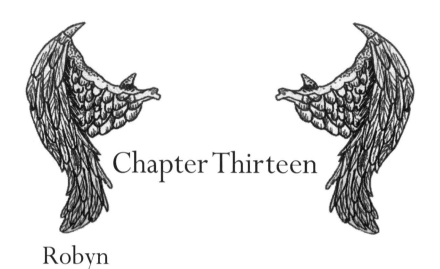

Chapter Thirteen

Robyn

Dylan stood there with roses in one hand and his phone in another. Clearing my throat, he smiled and put his phone in his back pocket before walking in. Without taking off his shoes he went straight to the living room and jumped on the sofa. I took a deep breath and walked in after him. He patted the sofa next to him and smiled, a new sense of charisma had formed in him. I placed the flowers in a vase that stood on the mantel piece and proceeded to sit formally beside him. Springing up beside me, he leaned in and gently kissed me on the cheek. As a gut reaction I flinched but instantly regretted my decision.

"Sorry," I said involuntarily. I could not help it; it was now a part of my subconscious. It had been embedded in my mind that I needed to apologize for fear that he was going to act out, to get angry with me and lash. He did not respond; he just smiled and continuing kissing down my neck and onto my collarbone. I believed he just ignored my apologies. I try to fight but cannot help the tears that start to stream from my eyes as I am frozen with fear. My muscles are trying not to seize but with every kiss he places on my body I tense. He pulled away Analysing me before hugging me awkwardly, testing if this would make me stop. I could not move.

"I-I'm sorry, I'm sorry I'm ignoring, you I just don't feel like it tonight. I actually have something I want to talk about." He raised an eyebrow and smirked sarcastically. The hairs on my

back now stood up, and I felt something twist in my stomach.

"Are you sure baby, you're normally always up for it." He

played with the gold chain my mum had left me that sat on my

neck. His fingers were fiddling with my bra strap. I was starting

to shake and I pulled away. He huffed; I could tell he was

starting to get irritated. I had to break up with him or this

nightmare would never be over.

"C'mon baby" He started kissing down my neck and running

his hands on my stomach and up my top.

"Dylan I really don't like it" He ignored my request and started

to move his hands down. Struggling, I started kicking and

opened my mouth to scream, he covered my mouth. I was

really starting to panic now. If Murdoc was supposed to

protect me where was he? When he told me, he had to go he

told me to be careful. Why the fuck did I tell Dylan to come over, this was my fault. I kicked even more in a chance he might hear me I screamed in my head,

"MURDOC HELP!" I was kicking now whilst Dylan continued to progress further. I placed my feet under his stomach and using all my force I pushed him so hard I thought my legs were going to snap. To my surprise he flew to the other side of the room crashing to the floor and into a plant pot that smashed upon collision. I held myself too scared to scream. Dylan got up clutching his arm that was dripping in blood from the underside of his arm.

"You are fucking BITCH!"

"Just please leave!"

He laughed.

"You are so fucking boring! You know what fuck you. I was just trying to make it up to you and you had to go all batshit crazy on me! We're fucking over, FUCK YOU!" He stormed out punching pictures on the wall before slamming the door so hard a small segment of plaster fell from the ceiling. I sat there frozen before the tears started streaming. I held myself trying to comprehend what just happened. I sat there for 30 minutes trying to calm myself down and think rationally about this.

"Murdoc please, if you're there, or you can hear me please talk to me."

Nothing.

I stood up dodging the soil and bits of ceramic, edging through the house I noticed mum's picture now laid on the floor surrounded by glass. Holding the picture up between my fingers I held it close to my chest. I wanted to be in her arms again. I want her, why did she go? why was she fucking driving! She knew she was not able to drive. Why did she allow herself? I ran upstairs and chucked myself in the shower

I needed any trace of him off me. I wanted it to go. The steam soon rose up filling the room, the window was closed and so was the door. Windows were now clouded in a thick fog of steam, sitting in the shower letting my fingers wrinkle, I did not want to leave; I could not go out again, it would mean I would have to face reality.

I turned off the water and sat in the bottom of the shower letting the steam dissolve around me, I curled my body up too ashamed to move. More than anything I wanted to be alone, but then I wanted to feel the comfort of everybody I loved. How would I tell dad about the plant pot or the picture?

Just as I was about to rock myself to sleep, I heard a blood-curdling scream.

Chapter Fourteen

Robyn

Loud banging brings me back to my senses. It was hard and heavy making the whole building shake, I had never heard someone knock this loud neither would I see the need to. What they were here for was a mystery to me, perhaps the neighbours had called as they heard something being smashed, although I was not close with my neighbours, but we still would help each other out if it were needed. We had friendly hellos or 'how're you?' but apart from those rare occasions we did not speak. I expected dad to open the door but it sprung upon me that he had gone on that business trip, I was the only one here.

"Police!" They shouted, knocking the door again. I pried myself out of the bottom of the shower. It occurred to me that I had slept in here and had the most awful dream that someone was screaming. Wrapping myself in a dressing gown that hung on the bathroom door I walked down the stairs to once again get pulled back to the events that took place yesterday. Broken glass consumed the hallway. The golden frame that hung so proudly on the wall was now on the other side of the room, cracked. They banged again and explained they have the right to force entry if incumbent.

"Come in! But be careful there's glass on the floor." I dumped myself on the steps, pulling my knees closer as the door opened. The sound of crackling glass came as the policeman strode in. They were both males, one had a very long beard and moustache wrapped over his mouth the one that stood next to him looked almost bald, no hint of a stubble appeared. He looked to his friend and signed dodging the broken pieces of glass as they circled the room with their gaze before concentrating it on me their sense of authority had now dropped to pity. In yesterday's events I could not recall if I had called the police, it was a possibility but a slim one. I had not looked in a mirror nor did I have time either nor did I care how I looked. The interrogative sentence still stood about why they were here in the first place. I presumed they were called for noise violations but would one smash of glass, well two, provoke the need for police. Would it not have been more appropriate to come last night not the morning after? Their eyes locked on me and with only a dressing gown covering my naked body I pulled it tighter.

"Are you Robyn skinner?" They asked, something hid behind their eyes. The policeman moved towards me not taking his eyes off mine, he had a touch of worry in his eyes, the faintness of a smile stood under his lips and lines of worry had formed across his forehead. In response, I nodded slowly. They probably thought I had gone mental, expressionless with a smashed-up house. I was surprised they have not tackled me to the ground. Flinching when they held out their hand helping me down, he pulled away studying himself before lowering his hand.

"It's okay, we just have some news, and we need you to answer some questions at the station." This was news to me. What did they possibly need questioning for? I hoped to god it was not anything to do with dad, the worst-case scenario braced my mind. I turned to go upstairs and quickly smeared on some deodorant threw on some clothes and shoes then walked back downstairs to see they were walking through the house, writing things on paper and taking samples of blood in the living room floor. I cleared my throat, grabbing their attention, whipping their heads around and staring at me.

With one last observational gaze around the living room, they instructed me to follow them out to the vehicle. The sky looked a dismal grey, I did not know the time and realized I had also left my phone stationed somewhere down the sofa. I had never ridden in a police car, it had never been an aspiration of mine, I felt ashamed to even be in a police car. Although I was not in trouble the atmosphere and series of events played out just like an episode of Coronation Street.

*

The room was cold, no heater was in sight, white brick walls formed a small square and the two officers had paper in front of them supposedly with a list of questions they were going to ask. I had done nothing wrong, so I was not troubled, but the question remained why I was here in the first place. I had been stationed at a small wooden table, I was conveniently provided a cup of tea and a pillow if I required.

"Do you know a boy named Dylan Roberts?" He questioned glancing up from his paper.

"Yes." I responded. So, this was not about my dad. What had happened with Dylan, surely no one knew about the incident. I could not bring myself to say the word. And surely, he would not go to the police for me kicking him as he would have got himself locked up for attempting to do *that* to me. He scribbled something down on a piece of paper before returning his gaze to me.

"What's your relationship with him?" He asked whilst scratching something out of his beard.

"I was his girlfriend. He broke up with me."

"When did you last have contact with him?"

"Last night." I regretted letting him into my home.

"Can you tell me the events that took place from the time he arrived at your house till when he left please," He had his pen ready and the thought of relaying the events that happened last night made me choke on my own spit. I spluttered, he pulled a tissue from the box that sat at the corner of the table and gave it to me and urged me to take my time. A few minutes later when I had composed myself, I told them the events that happened, and they listened to me passing tissues and getting me fresh cups of tea.

"Okay, well thank you for telling us. I'm sorry that happened to you but that does lead us to why we are here, Dylan Roberts and an unidentified female were found dead in a car last night."

The words seemed to stop and rattle around my head. Dylan was dead.

"What was the cause?" I asked, I did not feel anything upon asking this. I did not feel anything for him anymore.

"At first, we believe it was a suicide from looking in the window, we were only patrolling when we saw someone leaning against the steering wheel of the car. When we looked closer, we saw the female passenger and the violence of the scene. We instantly acquired the knowledge that it was murder. But an unusual one." He explained taking brief second breaks and then carrying on again.

"Why am I here?" I questioned, surely, they did not think I did it. How could I?

"Well, we ran his licence, found out his identity then looked on security cameras to find that the last person he was in contact with was you before the attack, so we just wanted to run a few questions by you to see the state of mind he was in, maybe he got into a fight on the way out." I knew what he was trying to do. He believed that I had something to do with it. Who would not think that? A girl almost gets raped, and now he has been murdered. Makes sense. But they had no evidence. If they had footage of Dylan leaving my house, they would see I did not leave either.

"Do you have footage of where he ended up and how he got there, maybe who did this?" I interrogated; I kept my cool. To be quite frank I did not care about Dylan. I wanted him dead, he cannot hurt anyone else now.

"We did, but it didn't pick up much, he drove out of your drive and then met the female in a parking lot, it seemed as though they got some food, then they stopped at the side of the road. A figure seemed to jump onto the car. It seemed as though it came from a tree. Wrapped in a hoodie. We are thinking it was most likely a male, then he attacked them. If you are stable, we do have pictures of the aftermath of the attacks. We do warn you though they are very graphic." He explained he grabbed glossy printed out pictures and waited for my nod of approval. I nodded on cue. Sliding the pictures towards me, I studied them.

"As you can see it was quite a violent attack. Unusual for this location, crime rates have been lowest this year." He said, the pictures had been taken at multiple angles, some far up, some really close in showing the smallest of blood splatters. The car was missing a door and the inside looked like it had been squeezed. Blood was everywhere, Dylan was in the driver's seat. The next series of photos mainly spotlighted him. His face had been beaten in showing broken bones distributed on the floor beside and in front of him. Clumps of hair were on his shoulders having been torn from his skull that had pieces of the bone with it. Teeth were snapped off and lodged in the side of his head, and it looked as though some fragments of bone had been shoved in his face and eyes. It made me cringe and felt my bones invert as I looked at the contortment Dylan's body had been put into. Even the most skilled of contortionists would not be able to achieve. I had only a few more photos to go but the next one I turned over was the worst by far. Dylan was laid on the steering wheel and his ribs had been pulled out from his chest and stuck into the muscle of his back to resemble wings. I studied it for a moment.

"it resembles something similar the blood eagle, used by the Vikings as a way to put someone to death." The police officer spoke as I studied the photo longer, I traced my fingers over it before pushing it aside. Turning over the next one it was of the female occupant, it appeared as though this was a different

223

investigation all together. She did not have nearly as many cuts or scratches on a single bruise across her neck and mouth.

"She died due to suffocation, we think, hence the bruises." He spoke again. The next photo was her face, something about her face sprang a memory I tried to put it together in my head, the ginger hair and the puffer jacket,

"I know who this is." I claimed to be pointing at her face even though it was clear who I was talking about. They edged closer in their seats.

"Brooke." I confirmed, pushing the remaining photo aside I watched them scribble the name down on the piece of paper in **bold**.

"Do you know her last name?"

"No."

"What was your connection with her, tell us anything you know it could really help figure out who the perpetrator was."

I rummaged through my head to retrieve any information I knew about Brooke.

"She's in my year at school, she had a boyfriend the last time I saw her, rumour has it that she sleeps with a lot of people, is very protective over her reputation and doesn't like being corrected and shown up." I had nothing to hide and neither did she now. They looked at each other, as though I was telling jokes and did not bother writing anything down.

"Right. Do you know if there is anyone, anyone at all, that would want to hurt either Dylan or Brooke? This was a very personal attack. Nothing was robbed from the car and comparing the attack of Brooke to Dylan it seemed as though the perpetrator had a much more intent to cause anguish to Dylan. They wanted to cause him pain compared to Brooke where they had just supposedly asphyxiated her. We think to lower the number of witnesses." He explained repeating himself multiple times and using hand gestures to try and explain. He scratched his moustache intriguingly.

"No, I don't. I had met her new boyfriend only once when I was working, but he didn't seem like the 'murderer' type." I raised an eyebrow. I had an itch that Murdoc had something to do with this but if it was him why not stop Dylan assaulting me in action.

They stacked their papers together tidily before speaking again, "Thank you, Robyn, really you have given us great information. Feel free to call this number if you need any more support or have any more information." He slipped me a piece of paper with numbers scribbled on it with a biro pen.

They drove me home, pulling up to my house. I took a minute before exiting the car.

Walking inside I was met with the mess of my house, carefully treading over the glass I retrieved my phone from the living room settee. Fifteen missed calls were from Maisie and over one hundred texts. She rang again,

"OMG YOU PICKED UP, WHERE ARE YOU HAVE YOU SEEN THE NEWS!" She screamed, almost breaking my phone speaker.

"Yeah, I just got back from the police station they had me in for questioning." I said,

"Can I come round, or do you need some time?" She asked, breathing heavily, recovering from her hysterics. I glanced around the house. It was not that bad, and I could have it cleaned by the time she got here, the living room would be tricky especially cleaning up the blood stains.

"I'm doing okay Maisie; I'd love to see you." She hung up, and I got straight to work first cleaning the soil and bits of sharp pottery then hoovering several times in the living room where the glass could have travelled too.

Whilst cleaning the hallway I heard the letterbox fly open and a small note was passed through the door, intrigued I crept over the glass to retrieve it, it read:

I am sorry this happened. I am sorry I came into your life and fucked it up. I will be leaving now, so I can live with my brother Elliot. We are just not compatible, we are worlds apart. It will not work. I am bound by rules that do not allow me to see you or talk to you anymore. We both have different wants and needs so trying to talk to you too makes things work would be a waste of time. Goodbye, Robyn.

-Murdoc.

Chapter Fifteen

Murdoc

Red discoloured the water. It had stained my hands leaving them a cold pink. The colour dissipated as the ripples carried the blood away. I had pulled a muscle during the attack, but it was worth it, she meant everything to me and now nothing could come between us. That girl might not have deserved to die, but at the same time she was a key witness and had the police on call. I silenced her as quickly and as humanly possible, breaking her neck. She did not fight it and merely sat there after I crushed her phone. She did not fight, but she refused to take her eyes off me when it happened. That is now embedded in my memory. Washing the remainders of blood from under my nails I heard the flapping of Elliot coming in close behind. I had not found him at the tree and after asking around the kingdom no one had seen him in days, I believed at some point I was being followed.

"Hey! Murdoc! I've been trying to find you everywhere!" He said coming behind and hugging me tightly.

"Where have you been?" I snapped, with the events that took place earlier today I did not want to play these games or put up with Elliot's charisma. He lost his grip and stepped back a few paces thinking. The fact he was thinking about it made me distressed, he had to think a lot when he was about to lie so whatever he was going to say was going to be taken with caution.

"You know, here and there." He chuckled. Maybe a bit too much as he was now giggling at his own laughter.

I pushed myself up with my hands on my knees still with my eyes fixed on the lake, it stood still watching us and judging me for disturbing it with the bloodshed. Mine and Elliot's tree only stood only a few hours away having another lake near it. When I had searched the tree looking for Elliot it seemed abandoned and carvings of a woman and violent acts being done to her lay carved into the bottom of the trunk.

I was now close to Robyn's house. I had planned to go back and wake her up and warn her about what I had done, but she was not in her bed. Then I heard the sirens, so I fled to the nearest lake, I needed to wash the evidence off me.

"I did it; I killed him." I said, still refusing to face him. He paused.

"I didn't think you would." He said sarcastically. He walked in a circle kicking the grass slightly and the flowers that grew under his feet as he walked. I turned slowly to face him. Looking older than when I had last seen him it seemed he'd had a growth spurt. His blonde hair had grown unruly, it had formed shaggy curtains that contrasted with his eyes that cast dusted freckles across his face. Hints of scaring slashed from his upper cheek bone to the right corner of his lip. Distressed jeans gripped his legs, once hanging loose, now ripped at the thighs. The white shirt that he was adamant he kept clean as it was his best piece of clothing now hung on him in threads, beaten and milky grey in colour.

"My job is to protect her and that is what I did." I stated, standing my place and making sure my tone reflected that.

Something had changed within Elliot it seemed as though he now hated everything. The laughter had slipped from his eyes, his friendly comfort had grown darker, they now resembled a dirty gold unlike the one that had sparked even in the darkest of rooms only a few days ago. His pupil's looked miniscule a tiny black dot in the sea of gold.

"Look, she's safe now so just leave her and stop with this ridiculous dream about running away with her. You cannot ditch me. You can't ditch Enlarnoc for this girl."

"Enlarnoc ditched us. What has happened to you? Why can't you just be happy for me." I snapped.

He gripped his fist and kicked the ground.

"Mum would be happy for me, I talked to the elder healer she told mc so herself."

"Well mum's not here anymore!"

He knew he had stepped too far when he said that because he loosened his grip and started pacing anxious for my response. I had a choice here; shout back or stay calm. I chose to stay calm. The last thing I wanted to do was pick a fight with Elliot. He smirked and then laughed to himself a malicious, evil, condescending, selfish laugh.

"What did you do?" I questioned walking towards him, and my fists scrunched. He was still laughing ignoring my question. His laugh made me uneasy and made me feel like throwing up. I knew he had done something to Robyn. He wanted to hurt me for some reason, and he knew Robyn was the most important thing to me, so of course that's what he went for. Why though? I had done nothing wrong. He knew I was searching for her, if he did not like it why help me find her in the first place? I marched over to him grabbing him by the shoulders and shaking him violently until he stopped laughing. My eyes pierced his demanding and answer. He loosened from my grip and took off into the sky. Confused I followed him, he flew into the trees. Feeling the bracing of thorns and twigs scratching at my face I pulled up hoping to get a better look from the sky, he had had the same idea and was almost miles ahead of me just over the second mountain. I tried to get through to Robyn, to tell her something had come up, that would keep me away for god knows how long, but she had blocked me out, whatever he had done had now destroyed her. I could not get through. Elliot flew through a cave over a mountain and then out of sight. I searched for days without any luck, no trace of him was left behind. Whatever he was planning he wanted to keep it a secret.

Chapter Sixteen

Robyn

"Let's go clubbing!" Maisie's enterprise clapping her hands together and squealing delightfully. I stared at her studying her face and why she was so excited before answering,

"Maisie please I don't feel like it-"

"C'mon Robyn! It's been almost a week now, and after you told me what he did fuck him, don't let him leave you like this." She cut me off with her positivity, it was not Dylan that had kept me from going out it was Murdoc. That note cut deeper, it seemed as though the only person that told me he would always protect me had now left. He could not even tell me himself. I believe that is what crushed the most. Everything seemed like a void now, dad had still not come back. His boss told me he would have to stay resident there for almost a year if he wanted to earn this promotion. My phone bill had officially run out as dad now had to pay for his own accommodation and was struggling to pay for the house and a hotel. The good news was that mum's picture had been restored to its original glory on the wall, but it never felt the same, she had picked out the frame that she wanted to be used for a family portrait, now it had a crack running through the frame that Maisie and I had made a poor attempt at painting over.

"Is this about Murdoc? You heard the doctor, he said it was just hallucinations from your recovery, you are better now. It is time to get out there! Celebrate your life, you almost got hit by a car for fuck sakes." She threw her arms around me and kissed my forehead leaving a black lipstick mark on my head that I ran to the bathroom to wash off before it stained. I reluctantly agreed to go out just this once, and she promises not to bug me about it again. They say getting ready for the club is the most enjoyable part of a party. It normally involves destroying some girl's bathroom and getting tipsy, so you do not have to pay for a lot of drinks when the bar opens. Maisie had brought me a dress from her house, it was black with a lace cut-out down the front that I had put over a pair of safety shorts. Although Maisie had tried to convince me to go commando, I had stood my ground but then crumbled and settled for wearing a thong underneath the shorts. Maisie did my makeup, powdering my face adding too much blush and winged eyeliner. She added a few small gems under my eyeliner that she claimed made my eyes sparkled and that my makeup would glow in the dark.

The taxi pulled up almost on cue, I felt surprisingly excited. I had not been clubbing for as long as I could remember and the last time, I ended up getting shit-faced and woke up in a field by a dog licking me in the face. Perhaps Maisie was right, and this was a new beginning. I wanted to get drunk and dance my way into the night then go home eating cheap junk food and then fall asleep on Maisie's bedroom floor.

Arriving at the club, lights were spilling out of the windows and the doors resembled a white canvas left in the hands of an artist, upon the sight of the building it gave me so many new ideas I could use for different paintings. The ideas came one after another, and I hoped the booze would not relinquish them from my memory. Feeling the vibrations of the music under my feet Maisie takes my hand and swerves through the sea of people to the bar where she ordered us a row of shots. The lights were rapidly changing certain to give someone an epileptic attack. The good vibes flow like a virus, a good one of course. Half the girls are wearing tops small enough to resemble bikinis and made me feel slightly overdressed. My hair had been straightened removing any curls, giving me a more sophisticated look. Maisie on the other hand looked wild, she wore a bralette with a fishnet top over and a leather glossy skirt. However, there was a steadiness to her like the storms passed over her head and instead of shying away from the rain she ran outside with her arms wide open. She was a rare woman, chaotic if not chaos herself but seemed to organize the chaos and let it come out attracting everyone to her. Two boys pulled up alongside us, they gave a smile and offered to buy us drinks, we took the offer without question. Even if we are not going to flirt with them some free drinks would be appreciated, sure it was unethical but that was the last thing on my mind right now. After finishing some shots, she dragged me to the middle of the dance floor right next to the speakers. I was starting to wonder if Maisie had taken me to a gay club as there were two men in the corner kissing. The pink skulls on her wheelchair lit up the floor, she pointed to my makeup that also seemed to glow in the dark. The club is electric tonight, we are all feeling the music travel through us. The music blurs around me, I am just feeling the beats radiate through my feet traveling up to my brain. With my drink in one hand and the other one above my head swaying to the music, I am in a moment of pure bliss. I could go like this all night long; the rainbow lights are fading all around us igniting smiles in the darkness. My feet are a puppet to the music, I do not know where the floor is anymore or the walls, people are now just blurring like me. Were all puppets being controlled by the auditory sensation. The songs are from our childhood and we are all singing and reminiscing our years of youth. I am dancing like it is my last night on earth.

With the euphoria wearing off I leave Maisie in the spotlight and try and claw my way to the bathroom. Whilst waiting in the colossal line for the girl's bathroom hard hands grab my waist and pull me towards them. They are unbelievably strong almost crushing my ribs. spinning around my eyes meet theirs. They are golden, almost full if it were not for a small black pupil hiding in the middle. I have never seen eyes like this, like golden embers. It was a man, the most noticeable thing about him other than his eyes was a scar running from his cheekbone to his lip. His presence felt strange like something wasn't right. Indistinguishable words floated and rattled around my brain as I tried to make sense of them,

Run.

Having no other options, I fled, crouching into the crowd I feel the man reach for my dress pinching the fabric, but it slipped through his fingers, Maisie's still on the dance floor I do not believe she is noticed I have gone, yet I can only imagine the panic she would feel when she sobers up. Running out of the club and almost falling down the metal ramp I flee down the road and become a victim to the night. The streetlights are the only source of direction I have. I wonder the perspective of the chaser, to him I am the prey, the lamb. It has been raining and freezing cold leaving the ground a frosty death-trap for anyone without a grip on their shoe, without a jacket the cold soon takes its toll aching my lungs and making it harder to breath. I can see my breath forming as it leaves my mouth, I remember doing this when I was a kid and pretending to be a dragon. I believed we all did this, then you had the wannabe gangsters who thought they were Kurt Cobain that pretended to be smoking. Footsteps were coming in close behind me. If I fail now my whole body will pay the price, I must keep going I have to push on.

Go to the bridge.

The bridge? Yes, the bridge! I dogged under the streetlights and then round the corner to where I found the big metal bridge that crossed over a powerful stream filled with rocks. The footsteps were louder now. The voice had disappeared, and I was trapped.

"There's no point running Robyn!" The man shouted panting slightly.

"How do you know my name?" I shouted back slowly walking away.

"Haven't you worked it out little girl?" He questioned laughing.

No, I have not. I have no idea who you are, so you should leave me the fuck alone.

"Fine, I'll explain it. I am Elliot, Murdoc's brother. You took him from me know I'm going to kill you, so I can have him back." He explained

"What? What are you talking about?"

"Fucking hell your thick. The guy who pushed you in front of the car that was me! But my stupid brother decided to risk Enlarnoc for you. Romantic right? And the note 'Murdoc' gave you, that was me! I was there when you went shopping, I was the guy in the hoodie." Enlarnoc? I tried to put the pieces together, but nothing was making sense. Nothing.

I gave a blank stare.

" Forget it. The Point is You took my brother from me, so now I am going to take you from him. It's that simple." He pulled out a knife and walked towards me.

Jump off the bridge.

"ARE YOU FUCKING INSANE?!" I called to him and the voice in my head.

Jump, quick!

I climb onto the metal barricades my heels teetering on the edge, Elliot was walking closer to me now. I had to just jump. Looking down I saw the crashing of water on the rocks, it was shallow water, if I were to jump I would die. Elliot was almost slicing at my heels I took a deep breath, closed my eyes and jumped.

The wind whipped my hair back. I felt splashes of water hitting my ankles.

Just then arms clasped around my waist and I felt the intensifying splashes of water become further and further away. Opening my eyes, I am high into the sky just below the clouds and I can see the whole town, it was beautiful. I went through trees and flew over rivers not wanting this feeling to stop but the air was crisp up here and with no coat I felt my body shaking. We started to slow down near a wood that bent around a small road. We end up slumped at a tree. The woods shrouded in mist. I glance up to see a young man about my age, big build with grey-blue eyes. He was gorgeous. Shaggy brow hair fell in his face and I lay on his chest feeling his warmth radiate through me.

"You're him? You're Murdoc?" He looked down upon me and a single tear fell from his eye.

"Yes Angel." He confirmed. I hugged him, and he pulled me close before picking me up and spinning around lifting me off the ground. He was a lot taller than me and I fitted just underneath his shoulder perfectly. Although we had never spoken, I felt more comfortable than ever, everything felt right.

I did not realize I was crying.

"You're real!" I exclaimed, hugging him tighter.

"It's okay Angel, I'm real."

"But the note...the note!" It all made sense Murdoc had not written the note it had been that Elliot guy. He hugged me tighter, his wings shielding me. I ran my hands along them feeling the feathers between my fingers. Tilting my chin up he leaned closer I felt his breath on mine, he was so close. Rain dropped onto my head and ran down my face.

"There's a hotel nearby and you're freezing, we need to get you somewhere warm, we should get going" He smirked as he pulled away, I pushed him playfully, he turned away laughing, "You little..." I trailed off noticing he was laughing too loud to listen.

He walked away, I followed him like a puppy to catch up, shielding me from the rain he lifted his wing up like a velvet umbrella. The moonlights out now casting the only light we need to get through the forest. Murdoc's patrolling the area with his eyes looking out for Elliot if he were to have followed us.

A crack of a twig signals our attention, to our left a stag stops and stares the black eyes cut through the mist. Murdoc raised a smile, flaring his wings to the stag that crept towards him, taking caution with every step. The stag had antlers vast and powerful, pointing upwards as if they were saluting the trees. His wet black nose reflected the moonlight leaving a shine like school shoes. With the wind nipping at my arms, I longed to go inside, but I had never seen a stag this close before, only at wildlife centres, I suppose that does not count. He creeps towards the stag and, bows? The stag seems to accept this and bows back his horns stretching along the ground, inspecting Murdoc by sniffing his black jeans then looking over to me. I try to stand as still as possible hoping I do not scare away this beauty of the forest, offering my hand gently the stag sniffs my fingers tickling them slightly before letting me stroke him. I never imagined what their coat felt like, but it was slightly rough and matted. Their horns have slight bumps like tree bark, fumbling under my fingers. Murdoc places a hand on my shoulder and kisses me gently on the cheek. My stomach flipped, leaving my heart to skip a beat. I wanted to take a picture, to frame this moment. I had been so engrossed I had not noticed the rain had now stopped leaving only a few droplets sliding off the leaves and dropping onto the woodland floor. My heels were holding up but I was conscious that the heel was about to snap from the slight uneasiness of the balance I felt standing up from this magical moment. The stag scampered from my uprise and fled into the forest

"You're adorable," He said giving me an almighty back hug.

"I didn't do anything." I said holding his hands tighter.

"You just are, okay." He gave a small chuckle and kissed my neck before kissing my head lightly. I turned to face him but shuddered as the frost scraped my heels. He pulled me closer and drew his wings around me, it was like leaning against a radiator. He wrapped his arms around me and kissed my head slightly.

"We need to get you to that hotel Angel. You are freezing. I don't know how good the hotel is so if its crap doesn't blame me okay." He laughed again and picked me up, so my head was now on his shoulder. He carried me all the way through the forest checking in with me every few minutes to make sure I was okay. I am pretty sure I fell asleep as when I woke up the hotel lights were now in sight. He propped me down knowing I had now woken up and held my hand as we crossed the road. I did not know the time still I suspected it was late as the street lamps were on and as bright as ever. No lights were on at the hotel except for the reception.

Chapter Seventeen

Robyn

Stodging into the hotel the first thing I noticed is that it was quite run down. Not hotel hell worthy, the walls were chipped, and the ceiling was peeling but they did offer a breakfast bar and other tea and coffee making facilities. Looking back to Murdoc I saw his wings had disintegrated leaving a trail of smoke following behind him. He glanced around then focused his gaze on me reluctant to acknowledge his surroundings. Pulling a roll of notes from his back pocket he placed it in my hand and whispered,

"I've never done this before." He admitted.

Walking across the hotel floor to the front desk I feel the heel on my shoe now coming loose as I had suspected. I was freezing, and it did not seem like the hotel had any better heating. Upon arriving at the desk, I started fiddling with the tightly wrapped roll of notes through my fingers. Looking back from her screen that displayed a gaze of Candy Crush. The receptionist gave me a rehearsed smile. She had a red floral top with small yellow flowers printed on it that matched her red rimmed glasses, a badge with the name; Carol came into view.

"Can I have a room with two single beds please?" I asked looking back at Murdoc who was inspecting the leaflets at the desk taking his time reading every page. He kept his head down, undercover with his hoodie casting a shadow over his eyes. The receptionist chewed her gum making large chewing sounds that made me want to punch the desk. Clicking off her game for a second she typed something into the computer, although she seemed to just be typing in random words, she looked back and squinted at me.

"No," She said, dragging out the 'no' just a bit.

"We've got a room with a double bed?" She said, still squinting at me.

"Yeah, that's fine." I responded. It was not. Having almost just met this guy I worried about sharing the same bed as him, however we did almost kiss back there. She typed something on the computer and I calculated the requested amount of money for one night. I turned to leave and heard a forced cough behind me. Gripping Murdoc's hand and dragging him away from the leaflets, through the halls and up the stairs acknowledging the numerous paintings of the seaside that scattered about the walls it did not seem to fit in with the decor, also seeing as though we were not near the seaside it seemed pointless. We got to room 287 and stood there for about two minutes attempting to get the key card to work. After trying for what seemed like another hundred times we pushed through and scanned the room. It had a TV, bed and a small kettle to make tea however there were no tea bags or cups. I turned to Murdoc, he was running his hands along the bed before springing himself upon it and sprawling himself out like a starfish he caressed the covers and nuzzled his face into it.

"Okay you have to give me some answers now." I said smiling and sitting beside him. He sat up and crossed his legs slightly bouncing on the bed like a toddler. The corners of my mouth would not stop upturning, they spread to the top of my cheek bones unable to force them down in his presence. Even though I was probably being hunted at this moment I did not care he made me feel safe.

"Well, I haven't got anything to hide now so what do you want to know." I think it was obvious what I wanted to know.

"Who was that guy who just tried to kill me?" I asked, he looked at me and started fidgeting with his fingers again the creases of a smile dulled.

"That was my brother, Elliot." He confirmed the same as the guy did back at the bridge.

"Why does he want to kill me?"

"I don't know, he's changed. One moment he is on board with the whole thing then the next moment he is trying to push you in front of cars. It doesn't make sense." He hung his head down, it was as if he was contemplating. I could see the cogs turning in his mind and whizzing round again.

"He said I took you from him?" I questioned trying to make sense of everything and piece it together.

"When we were kids, we had this great plan to escape Enlarnoc-"

"Enlarnoc?" I interrupted.

"It's where I was born, it's a kingdom. We have a king called Ragnus. So, we planned to leave, but now that Elliot sees you in the picture, he wants you out. He's always been very attached to me; it was just me and him for such a long time."

"I-I'm sorry. I feel awful. Why me? How did you even know I existed?" I wanted to know everything all at once, it was almost one in the morning, I bet Maisie was worried sick.

"Don't feel bad it's really not your responsibility, Elliot couldn't fathom that we could all have a life and if you were in it, he wouldn't be left behind. And I did not choose you as such. We get assigned 'soulmates'-"

"Wait just to clear something up, what are you?" He looked at me with a nipping grin.

"You really not caught on? Wings? Come from a kingdom? Human form?" He waited for me to get it and when I did not, he chafed his head pretending to be in pain from my dimness, "I'm an angel, well half angel. My dad's an angel and my mum was a human."

"Ohhhhhh!" I said slapping my knee at how obvious it should have been.

"So, as I was saying, angels get assigned soulmates and since I have that blood in me, I got a soulmate too. We do not know who they are and the closer we get to them the louder we can hear their thoughts. It is very rare for a human and an angel to get paired so when I could not hear anything in the kingdom I had to travel across water and towns for months to find you, then I heard you thinking about this Kurt Cobain guy, so I assumed he was your boyfriend…whatever, I was so close to finding you then I got kicked out by the guardians. That meant I had to tell Elliot where to find you. When he told me about Dylan, I had to come to find you and make contact." I was nodding my head but at the same time trying to put things together. He had done a good job at explaining it was just my job to process it. He placed his hand on my back and rubbed it gently. It sends a spark travelling up my spine. I shuddered and laughed heartily trying to draw attention away from my cheeks that had now become potent with red blush. This was different to Dylan he had a softness to his touch, a relief.

"Okay, so guardians are another angel?"

"There is a different type of angel, we have warriors' healers the lot." This world seemed so incredible, a kingdom full of angels, warriors and guardians. It was surreal I felt like the only human in the world that knew this place existed.

"So why couldn't you see me in person?" I asked. If his parents were human and angel why couldn't, he see me. Surely, they would be supportive of the idea? Murdoc looked at me and licked his lips before speaking,

"Ragnus has a rule that humans and angels aren't allowed to be together. My mum fell victim and my dad got banished." I do not want to know what 'fell victim' meant, I assumed it was not good. His dad had got banished meaning he was by himself. Where did Murdoc sleep? A uniform tear fell from his eye and slid down his face. Using my thumb, I whipped it away and his eyes locked with mine. Briefly those blue eyes showed a lifetime of struggle that could not be put into words. His eyes were the waves crashing against rocks, if you could imagine that, they were passion and held a companionship that would walk alongside you for life.

"I'm sorry that happened to you, I lost my mother as well, a car accident took her from me." He kissed me on the cheek gently restoring the smile that had slipped now, we sat in a present moment of grief just supporting each other. Rain was now smashing onto the windows stopping us from seeing the world that lay outside. My phone buzzed breaking the moment. It was Maisie. Murdoc, taking the hint, motioned and scuffled aside for a moment letting me have a few moments to inform Maisie about the events that had taken place.

"Hey Maisie! I'm okay, don't worry." The throbbing of the music was coming through the phone making it almost unbearable for me to hear her let alone anything she was trying to say.

"WHERE ARE YOU!" Although the music was almost in the background, she was supposedly outside, she was still yelling.

"I met him. Murdoc. He's real!" I overlapped a glance with Murdoc as Maisie screamed with excitement down the phone. He laughed full heartedly and investigated the bathroom further.

"I can't talk right now Maisie, but I promise I'll explain everything when I see you again. We're at a hotel right now."

"Oooo! Have fun but not too much fun." She said as she made kissy noises down the phone before hanging up. I sprawled out on the bed trying to remove the face of my attacker. Those eyes and that laugh, I do not understand how they could possibly be related. I could not seem to shake it.

Seeing Murdoc's hoodie and with him in the bathroom with the shower going I peeled out of the dress and now regretted wearing a thong. However, his hoodie was big enough to go down to my knees. I turned the main light off and switched on the two bedside lamps then crawled onto bed. My feet were killing from running in platforms, but it occurred to me that Murdoc had been having the longest shower, almost an hour to be exact. The clock was reading almost three in the morning when he appeared with a towel wrapped around his waist. Although his face was slim his waistline was slightly fleshy, not that there was anything wrong with that, more to love. I hadn't been fond of Dylan's 'rock hard abs' as he'd call it. It felt like hugging a piece of cardboard. Hugging Murdoc was like hugging a pillow, it was warm and comforting it made you feel safe. He stopped and examined me, looking me up and down as if he could see under the sheet that was covering my best assets.

"You don't mind, do you?" I asked tugging the hoodie. He removed the towl from his waist revealing a pair of black boxers and vigorously rubbed his shaggy hair with it. He threw the towel on the floor and just ended up shaking his head like a dog. I laughed feeling the water fly onto the bed and my face.

"Not at all." He said laughing at his own actions. He grabbed his t-shirt out of the bathroom and proceeded to pull it over his head, it fitted snugly. He needed a bigger size, I did not know if they had cloth shops in Enlarnoc or if he had got it from human villages. He climbed into the bed next to me and hugged the covers.

"I've never felt anything so soft in my life!" He said burying his head into the pillow, so that answered my question.

"I was meant to ask this earlier but where did your wings go?" I asked running my hands up his shirt and along his shoulder blades where the mighty wings had stood only a few hours ago.

"Because I am half angel, I can hide them, so can Elliot that how we can appear human. Good for getting away with things." He said with a grin. I ran my finger down his spine and when I went off to the side he flinched.

"What's wrong?" I asked moving my hand away.

"I'm ticklish, don't do that!" He said through his laughter. I laughed too finding it funny that this mythical creature that appeared so strong had a tickle spot. He turned over so he now had his back against the bed and used the pillows to prop himself up. I think it had now hit us that we were here. Me and him. To everyone he was my hallucination, but he was real. He scooted over, so our legs were now touching. I turned on my side to face him, although the silence was loud it was not awkward. We were both just enjoying life. Pushing everything away. He raised his hand, consequently I flinched slightly until he placed it on my cheek gently,

"Sorry, you're just beautiful. I've never met anyone like you."

He smiled, and I could see his eyes starting to water. I nuzzled into his hand not wanting this to end or for him to go away again. He parted his lips and leaned forward staring into my eyes and then smiling again before closing them. I leaned in waiting to feel his lips on mine, then it hit like a firework going off. We stayed like that not wanting this feeling to end before he pulled away slightly and licked his lips. He smiled and red blush seeped into his cheeks. Just as we were about to drop off we could hear the constant squeaking of a bed in the room above us, Murdoc and I burst into a fit of laughter. My lungs were aching from the laugher and Murdoc even managed to form a few wheezes during our fit. He had a unique laugh I fell in love with it and tried everything I could to keep him laughing and scrolling through my personal library for any jokes I could come up with. I scooted into his arms and nuzzled my head into his neck and kissed it gently. He flinched and laughed again; I am guessing this was another one of his tickle spots. I

kissed him on the cheek instead.

"Goodnight." I whispered into his neck.

"Goodnight Angel."

The reality still lay that his brother wanted to kill me, and

Murdoc had to choose.

Chapter Eighteen

Murdoc

Sun warmed my skin waking me from my dreams, Robyn lay

in front of me, her face was cast into sunlight. Her makeup still

had not washed off from yesterday leaving the pillows to have

a small smudge of foundation. I kissed her head gently and

traced my finger along her jaw. God, she was gorgeous. I lay

there for a minute watching her sleep and reminding myself

how lucky I am. Just to think if I'd never made contact, I

would not be here. I wished I had a camera to frame this moment, id print out the picture and keep it wherever I go.

Slowly her eyes open, and she smiles this amazing smile at me then leans in, she kisses me like it is the last day on earth. I kiss her back with the same energy, I have never experienced this before. I have never had a girlfriend. She kisses me gently and pulls away that leaves me with the cheekiest grin on my face. My breaths quickened and she is smirking.

"What?" She asks putting her hand on my chest making my breath quicken.

"I've just never really been kissed like that." I admitted giving her a worried smile, I did not want her to think I was not enjoying it because I was, trust me I was.

"Aww, was it okay or was that too much?" she asked a touch of worry behind her eyes. The last thing I wanted was for her to feel like I was like Dylan.

"No, No... I really liked it." I was stuttering even thinking about kissing her like that again. Desire took the best of me as I climbed on top of her and kissed her letting her know how much I liked it.

Leaving the hotel, I called a taxi for Robyn as I needed to find Elliot and the last thing I wanted was to get her involved with him again. I knew where I would find him, so I headed to the tree. With the events of this morning still red in my cheeks I now had a new passion. Elliot had a choice; he could stop all this and came with me and Robyn, or he would leave us alone for good. Abandoning my little brother is something I thought I would never have to do, but now Robyn was the most important thing to me since being assigned.

Reaching the tree, I saw Elliot slumped against it. Gracefully landing and vanishing of my wings I insinuated peace. I had never seen him look worse; he was humming a tune that our mother would sing to get us to sleep. His face was scratched up and his eyes were bloodshot. I sat beside him,

"What's got into you Elliot. You used to be so on board with the idea, and now you are trying to kill her? I don't know who you are anymore." He looked up and took a swig, I am guessing some sort of alcohol,

"I'm the one who changed? You ditched all of us!" He slurred.

"Look, you can come with us, me, you and Robyn, we can all go away together. Just like you wanted, but you've got to stop all of this nonsense." He laughed then stood up almost falling back.

"IT WAS ME AND YOU." He cried, throwing the bottle on the tree and smashing it. He stumbled with the remainder of the bottle in hand walking towards me. Cautiously I stumbled back. He was not going to hurt me. Not Elliot. All I see is

Elliott, literally. Everything falls away in a momentum behind us. He is swinging the weapon closer whilst crying, the tears burning his cheeks leaving scars. Blood now coming out of his nose and ears, I want to hug him, to bring him close and tell him everything is going to be okay, one hit to the stomach and I could be impaled and bleed out within minutes. He was coming closer swinging more vigorously almost tripping over and impaling himself in the process.

"Elliot it's me, put the bottle down." I plead. He was going to get someone hurt if I could not get the bottle from him. He laughed a malicious evil laugh and ran towards me swinging the bottle wildly. He pounced I grabbed his wrist with the bottle in it, he fought to pull it down and smash it into my head, the sharp shards were so close, and he had grown stronger. Tears fell from his eyes scorching his cheeks as he screamed and grunted trying to pull the bottle down. I thought of Robyn, that smile and fuelled that into my strength, pushing him off grunting I pulled his arm down and pulled him into me his body impaling into the remains of the bottle. At that moment I feel everything drain from my body. I crouch down letting him lay in my lap letting his head rest across my legs. Blood started to spill out his ears and soaked through his shirt where the bottle dug deep. He was gasping for air and a single tear fell from his eye.

"Hey. Look at those colours. Look up." I watched his eyes follow my gaze to the sky, it was sunset and had portrayed the most unfathomable colours into the sky, vibrant oranges and yellows and purples created a beautiful canvas. He stopped struggling and took one last inhale before the fire in his eye extinguished. I pulled him closer letting my head rest on his, my tears fell to his face washing away some of his blood.

Ten minutes stretched to forty, he lay in my lap. I had closed his eyes, so he could rest peacefully. I spent hours digging him a grave and then covered him in a bed of wild flowers that had rose under his feet whilst he had walked. I sat beside him talking to him and telling him about the adventures we had, I told him about mum cooking and then asking dad to send our food to the tree. We would camp in this tree and planned to build a fort but never got the time. Mum was gone and dad was out there somewhere, not knowing his son had died. I kept repeating over and over to Elliot that it did not have to end up like this, why had he not put the bottle down. I told him I was sorry. Words could not explain the sorrow I felt, my hands trembled, saturated in his blood reminding me again that I had killed my own brother. My own blood. What my mother died for.

I washed the blood off my hands and washed my clothes in the lake, trying to get the last of the stains out. It was me and Robyn now. She is all I have got left.

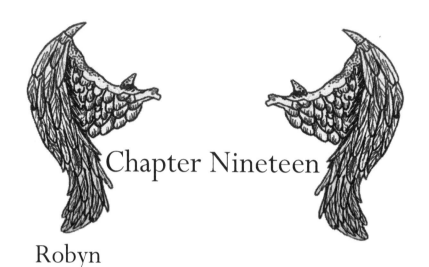

Chapter Nineteen

Robyn

Creaking from my window woke me from my sleep, I had seen

his face everywhere. Elliot's laugh rung in my ears and haunted

my dreams, I found myself checking over my shoulder more

recently and placed keys between my fingers in case of an

attack. Murdoc had been gone for three days, I was not

worried about him, I knew he would be able to take care of

himself. I not only feared my safety but for Maisie's and my dad's, I knew what he was capable of and according to Murdoc he was not the same person.

The windows creaked again and everything seemed real. I buried myself under the covers and felt the shadowy figure creep into my room and shut the window. The bed squeaked as weight got shared, a hand pulled back the covers leaving me vulnerable. I spun round to find Murdoc leaning over me, relieved I grasped onto him and buried my face into his chest. Breathing his scent in and feeling his comfort, he wrapped his arms around me and his wings followed casting a comforting darkness over us. He kissed my head softly. My hands brushed his wings, they were velvet folding over my fingers, Murdoc's eyes pierced the darkness showing light in our future. If you were to ask me now if I believe in soulmates; yes, yes, I do.

"Get your clothes on I need to show you something." He whispered brushing some hair out my face and kissed my forehead. I ignored the breeze that was nipping at my legs and quickly pulled on a pair of jeans and a hoodie. I checked the time, and it was almost six in the morning. I pulled on some socks and slipped into some comfortable shoes. Murdoc was inspecting my room looking at my paintings and canvases that were stacked up in the corner.

"Did you paint these?" He asked flicking through the canvases.

"Yeah. The one in the front, with the wings, kind of looks a bit like you." I said tying my shoelaces and pointing to the painting in front just in case he missed it.

"It's amazing Angel, I'm proud of you." He stood up and kissed me on the cheek before giving me a smile.

"Where are we going then?" I asked grabbing his hands and wrapping them around me.

"You'll see." He led me to the window by my hand. I watched him take his shirt off and two marvellous wings grew from his back stretching out like an extra pair of arms. He bent

forward.

"Get on." He commanded.

"What?" I questioned laughing at the idea of getting a

piggyback at this age.

"Trust me." He said grabbing my hand and helping me onto

his back, his skin was warm to the touch, I wrapped my hands

around his neck feeling his chest for a moment before

wrapping my legs around his hips. He walked to the window

and I buried my face in his neck, it was almost sunrise, I was

still in wonder of what he wanted to show me.

"Am I safe now? From him." I blurted, I could not help it, I

needed to know that I was free to be with him.

"You are safe Angel; I will kill anyone who tries to hurt you.

Anyone" He responded bracing himself out the window.

Feeling the cold breeze rush past my ears I clung tighter to Murdoc letting his warmth contrast the nipping of the wind. The streetlights were still on but dimming fast.

"Are you sure about this?" I asked scared he might fall even though it was completely irrational.

"Hold on Angel." He said, I felt his wings lift from the windowsill. And he took to the sky, I held on tighter knowing if I let go, I would end up a splat on the pavement. I could see the sun rising now, we trailed over the town climbing higher every second until we were flying over a lake the waves were crashing over each other causing consistent ripples. The lake led to a landscape of green hills upon hills building up to form a colossal mountain, it all seemed so small from up here. I had my arms outstretched Murdoc sped up moving his wings in big hard pushes ascending us higher into the sky to where we were almost reaching the clouds.

The wind stroked my face as we edged closer to the sun, the bright orange colours all forming the most gorgeous sunrise I had ever seen. It was as fresh as colours brushed upon an artist's canvas, a sky of fire and passion. My whole body felt free, I was here in the now, flying high above the world and nothing could stop me. I reached up to feel the clouds they slipped through my fingers. It was Murdoc and I, in this now, forever and always.

I leant back down wrapping my hands around him tight and kissed his cheek, I could not stop myself from smiling this was incredible. The sun was almost fully up now, I have always wanted to watch the sunrise with someone I love, but I never imagined it to be like this. Tears sprang from my eyes and fell onto his back but quickly disappeared.

What's wrong Angel? He asked through my mind, the wind was too loud to talk over.

"I've just never had someone treat me this well before."

I promise I am never going to hurt you. I love you Robyn.

"Always?"

Always.

THE END

The Wings That Follow Playlist

Here is a selection of songs that I believe fit selected chapters, a particular character or moment. Have a listen, who knows, you might find a few songs you like.

Elliot: Mr. Manson/ Max Diaz

Maisie: Bubblegum Bitch/ MARINA

Murdoc: Everlong/ Foo Fighters

Robyn: Sharpener/ Cavetown

Murdoc first finding Robyn: Lonely Eyes/ The Front Bottoms

Chapter Fourteen: Trash People/ Cherry Glazerr

Chapter Fifteen: Wolf in sheep's clothing/ Set It Off

Chapter Sixteen: Don't You Worry Child/ Swedish House Mafia, Incredible/ M-Beat

Chapter Seventeen: Yellow/ Coldplay

Chapter Eighteen: Cold Cold Cold/ Cage The Elephant

Chapter Nineteen: Can You Feel My Heart My Heart/
Bring Me The Horizon, Sparks/ Coldplay

Robyn & Murdoc's song: Please Never Fall In Love
Again/ Ollie MN

Acknowledgments

I always thought that writing acknowledgments would be difficult, finding words to say and how to say it and I was right. I do not understand how people can write pages and pages of acknowledgments, especially if you are self-publishing, and would not be surprised if someone were just to write a load of rubbish for this page as who really reads acknowledgments. Anyways, I guess I should start by saying thank you for my mum and dad for supporting me and a big shout out my mum for helping me format and design the book cover. I want to of course say thank you to Max for putting up with me going on tangents about this book and I hope this book finds you a love for reading and fantasy. I want to say how much I appreciate everyone who decides to read this book and support me. Thank you!

The Wings That Follow